COME, CATHERINE

When Catherine visits the Constantines at Treworgey, her stay is longer than she anticipated. She becomes involved in the lives of Aunt Ada, Mimsy and Uncle Lando, and doesn't want to leave. She agrees to a 'marriage of convenience' to the head of the family, Edward, intending to earn her place in the household. But when Paula Penlove returns to the neighbouring estate, she realizes that she loves her 'husband' — but is it too late to tell him so . . . ?

NINA LOUISE MOORE

COME, CATHERINE

Complete and Unabridged

LINFORD
Leicester

First published in Great Britain in 1974
Robert Hale Limited
London

First Linford Edition
published 2008
by arrangement with
Robert Hale Limited
London

Moore, Nina Loui

Moore,   Come, Catherine
Come   / Nina Louise
Linfo: Moore
1. Lo   LP
2. La
I. Titl 1827286
823.9

ISBN 978–1–84782–377–9

Published by
F. A. Thorpe (Publishing)
Anstey, Leicestershire

Set by Words & Graphics Ltd.
Anstey, Leicestershire
Printed and bound in Great Britain by
T. J. International Ltd., Padstow, Cornwall

This book is printed on acid-free paper

1

'Isn't this rather a sudden arrangement?' I asked Miss Marston doubtfully, when I called at the agency and she offered me a couple of weeks' typing for a Mr. Edward Constantine, of Treworgey House, Hawken — in Cornwall. Accommodation would be found for me, she said, and if I travelled down the next evening there would be someone to meet me at the station.

'It's just the job for you, and there's nothing shady about it: references were sent from Mr. Constantine's bank, via their branch here in Plymouth. I've given your name; you aren't going to let me down, are you? The trouble with you, Catherine, is that you're not adventurous.'

I knew Miss Marston quite well, I'd been on her list at the agency for several years and was ensured work that suited me: that is, jobs without shorthand at which I was hopeless, and not positions in large establishments where too much hustle and bustle would make me nervous and incompetent. She was right, I wasn't adventurous, but I wasn't going to refuse this work so I took the particulars and thanked her and went home to start packing. I shared a flat with another girl and as long as the rent was paid there was no difficulty about leaving, I would be back again soon; I'd had short-term jobs away from Plymouth before.

The next day was dull and rather cold for June, and by the evening as I journeyed into Cornwall heavy rain was falling; the dark leaves and pink blossoms of the rhododendron bushes lining parts of the railway embankment glowed with a kind of fluorescent brightness in the early-gathering dusk. My old mackintosh wasn't very waterproof and as I neared my destination I anticipated a soaking just walking up the station platform, but as soon as I got off the train a tall, elderly gentleman, wearing a caped coat like coachmen used to have, was standing over me with a large umbrella. 'Excuse me, you are Miss Kingsley?' he asked, and added, 'I'm Tom Pacey, from Treworgey House.' Perhaps I was the only likely-looking person from the train, for he had claimed me before he spoke.

'Yes, I'm Catherine Kingsley,' I said, and he took my suitcase and, sheltering me with the umbrella and warning me of the puddles to be avoided, led me up the platform. 'We have to find the station-master,' he told me.

I wondered why we needed to do that, for all the other alighting passengers had passed through the barrier in the normal manner. He explained: 'Mr. Edward said the station-master must identify me; must tell you I'm from Treworgey.'

'Oh, we needn't bother, need we?' I said, 'I'm sure you're who you say you are.'

'I must obey Mr. Edward's orders,' he replied emphatically. 'He said no young lady would want to drive off with a stranger she wasn't certain about.'

My new employer must be a careful man, or old-fashioned — or perhaps just thoughtful for others, for I could see the reason for such precaution and was reassured by it. The station-master came out of his office and at Mr. Pacey's request he said, 'Yes, Miss, this is Tom Pacey, Mr. Constantine's chauffeur.' He made it seem to be me who'd required the identification and that he thought me silly to need it.

There was a big black car in the station yard, I thought it was probably a Bentley, but as Mr. Pacey drove along the country road with me sitting in the back in splendid isolation I felt our vehicle was a Victorian carriage; I expect my companion's coaching cape gave this illusion. We didn't have any conversation but as we passed through what I took to be a small market town Mr. Pacey said, 'This is Treluz Major', and farther on when we came to a village he said 'Treluz Minor' and eventually, after a ten to fifteen miles ride from the railway station, he told me that a cluster of stone-built cottages and a few shops and a church was, 'Our village, Hawken.' I looked out to see all I could, thinking I would probably be lodging in one of these cottages for the duration of this job.

At the church we turned to the right down a narrow lane and after about a quarter of a mile came to Treworgey House. It was a large, solidly-built Victorian dwelling and seemed rather a dismal place in the rain, but inside I was to find all the comforts and conveniences of modern living. When Mr. Pacey had carried my suitcase into the hall he knocked on a door and in a few moments it was opened by a plump middle-aged lady. He said respectfully, 'This is Miss Kingsley, ma'am,' and he departed.

'Welcome to Treworgey, Miss Kingsley,' the lady greeted me, shaking hands, 'I'm

Mrs. Drummond — Ada Drummond. I keep house for my nephew, Edward Constantine. He thought you would like a quiet supper with me tonight and he will see you in the morning, so I'll show you to your room then you can come down and join me here when you're ready.'

'Am I to sleep at the house?' I asked, surprised.

'Of course. Where else? There's plenty of room.'

She took me upstairs to quite a large, very pleasant bedroom and left me to freshen up after my journey. I went to the half-open window and looked out over a rain-soaked garden; there were fields beyond and a screen of summer-green trees. Wood pigeons were cooing and the damp air carried the scent of roses and honeysuckle; it was very peaceful; I felt as if I'd come here for a holiday. I washed, then went down-stairs. Mrs. Drummond was waiting for me in a little sitting-room and we sat at a small table; our supper was brought to us by a lady of about the same age as

Mrs. Drummond. She was a tiny woman, short and thin, and was introduced to me as, 'Miss Mimms, who cooks for us.'

It was a nice meal; I was hungry and enjoyed it. As we ate, Mrs. Drummond explained: 'Besides my nephew, Edward, and Miss Mimms and myself — I'm a widow — there's my mother — we all call her Granny — and my brother, Orlando. I'd better warn you what to expect with Lando: he's not quite right in the head, through no fault of his own or of the family blood, poor man. He's harmless and you won't see much of him; he has his own rooms and a man — Victor — to look after him. He joins us for some meals; he's very fat — he overeats, but how can we deprive him of the pleasures of food when all the other good things in life are lost to him?'

'I'm sorry your brother is ill, Mrs. Drummond,' I said, feeling some such remark was necessary. 'Is there any hope of improvement?'

'No, none, I'm sorry to say. By the

way, you'd better call me Aunt Ada, like everyone else does; I shall hardly know who you mean if you address me as Mrs. Drummond.'

Miss Mimms brought in coffee and sat with us, she seemed to be one of the family. She and Aunt Ada had been at boarding-school together in the nineteen-twenties, they told me; Aunt Ada had come back to Treworgey to be a young lady of leisure and then to marry, but Miss Mimms had to earn her living and had studied domestic science and then taught the subject at a Plymouth girls' school. They had kept in touch with each other and later when Treworgey was in need of a cook Miss Mimms had filled the post. I found them a cheerful, chattery pair, but although it was summer they had switched on the electric fire 'to keep out the damp' and I was soon muzzy with the heat and the sound of their voices. I said I was tired and went to bed early rather than nod off to sleep in front of them.

2

The next morning I presented myself to Mr. Constantine in the library which led off from the little sitting-room where I'd had breakfast. He was sitting at his desk but stood up as I entered the room. There was a comfortable looking, chintz-covered chair beside the fireplace — it was the only easy chair there — but I sat in a small ordinary one facing him, which I thought the right place for an interview; however, this seemed wrong, almost as if I embarrassed him, for he moved to the fireplace and stood with an arm stretched along the mantelshelf, slumping a little as if he felt too tall for the room — he *was* tall, and sun-burnt and strong-looking, though not what would be considered handsome: I thought him nice. He was between thirty and forty years old. We'd exchanged a 'good-morning' when I came into the room and now, as he was silent, I decided I must speak again; I said: 'I'm ready for work.'

He laughed at that and asked: 'Is your room comfortable Miss Kingsley?'

I hadn't expected him to care if I was comfortable or not so I replied enthusiastically, 'Oh yes, it's lovely; like a posh hotel and with a view of the garden!'

He laughed again and stood there idly kicking at a white dog, a boxer, which lay on the hearthrug — the kicks weren't meant to hurt and the dog squirmed with pleasure as if at caresses.

Mr. Constantine appeared reluctant to get on with the interview but as I looked round the room wondering if this was where I would work and if I could manipulate the old-fashioned typewriter which stood in the muddle of papers on the desk he eventually began. 'This job may not be quite what you expected,' he said, 'and I hope you won't feel we've brought you here on false pretences. I'll explain: my grand-mother is ninety, but she's an extremely alert old lady and she knows and remembers more about Treworgey and Hawken and the country around than any of us. She tells us stories about the past but Aunt Ada and the others aren't interested and I haven't the time to take notice; yet I don't want it all to be forgotten when she's gone. I thought if you would talk to her, let her tell you what it was like here in this part of Cornwall in her young days, you could get it down on paper and type it out, just so there's some record of those times.

'For instance, there used to be an old man with a donkey and cart who came round selling ginger-bread — this would be about the turn of the century, I think; and another brought cheese tarts and mutton pies to the village; and there was a blind man who sold tea, loose tea to be measured into a caddy. She saw a German submarine sunk off the Point by our gunfire in the 1914–1918 war, and even remembers when sail boats came up the Creek at high tide, before it was so silted up with sand as now; and she knows what it was like here before the top road to Treluz Major was made, and when there was a horse bus to take people into Treluz Minor on Saturdays — things like that shouldn't be lost for ever.'

'It sounds very interesting,' I said. 'I'll do my best.' This would be different from my usual jobs which were generally dull copy-typing.

'Well, take your time; there's no hurry,' replied Mr. Constantine. Did he mean that the work was to take more than the two weeks I was engaged for? It would suit me if I was to be at Treworgey for the rest of the summer!

Someone knocked on the door and when Mr. Constantine crossed the room to open it Aunt Ada was there; she didn't come in but said in a worried voice: 'The television is wrong again, Edward. It was all wavy lines last night and I've checked again with the school's programme and it's still the same.'

'Ring up the shop! Don't bother me about it!' snapped Mr. Constantine impatiently. And then, more kindly, 'Will you take Miss Kingsley up to Granny now please, Aunt Ada?'

'Yes, certainly Edward,' she replied obediently, and she led me up to a room on the same landing as my bedroom but at the front of the house — my room at the back had a prettier view I thought; the view from Granny's room was of the gravel drive, the lane, and then the village, but included Hawken church and churchyard which, I learnt, was what she liked to look out on. This morning she was sitting near the window in a straight-backed chair; she was knitting what looked like a baby's jacket. 'Here's Miss Kingsley, Granny,' said Aunt Ada, and she crossed the room to kiss her mother and fussily adjust the cushion at her back; I could see this irritated the old lady for she immediately wriggled it into its former position again.

It was difficult to realize those two

were mother and daughter: Aunt Ada was pleasantly plump with middle-age and wore sensible country-life clothes and no make-up, and her thinning fair hair was fading to grey and grew in wispy, uneven strands; her mother, elegant even at ninety, was slim and wore a pretty flowered silk dress, her white hair was plaited round her head in a kind of crown, her not-too-wrinkled face was pink-powdered and her mouth lip-sticked into a coral cupid's bow that didn't seem out of keeping with her age. There was a delicate scent of violets in the room.

Granny waited till Aunt Ada had departed before speaking but then she greeted me sweetly, told me to sit down, and we talked together and got on well. I helped her to wind wool for the interminable pile of garments she was making for Oxfam and then she produced needles and started me on knitting too — large coloured squares for a patchwork quilt.

I met Orlando — Uncle Lando — in

the dining-room at lunch-time: he didn't answer when I said, 'How d'you do', and Aunt Ada said, 'Uncle Lando is feeling shy this morning, Miss Kingsley,' as if he were a bashful schoolboy instead of a middle-aged man not much younger than herself; as she had said, he was very fat — a soft, unhealthy fat which made him rather repulsive to look at. I sat opposite him and he beamed full-moon smiles at me throughout the meal, fascinated by a new face. I smiled back but was afraid to speak to him in case he wasn't able to understand, though he and Victor, his 'keeper', talked together at times; Uncle Lando's voice was an incongruous falsetto. I tried to ignore the greedy eagerness with which he eyed the food and the slobbering way he ate.

I was surprised that Victor was young; he was probably only in his early twenties. His dark hair was shoulder-length — I didn't like and couldn't get used to the long-haired style for men — and he looked to be starting a beard;

he had no conversation with any of us except the few sentences that passed between himself and Uncle Lando.

As I became accustomed to life at Treworgey I realised what a strange household we were. We lived separately most of the time: Aunt Ada and Miss Mimms — Mimsy, as I learnt to call her — had the kitchen and little sitting-room as their domain; Granny had her rooms on the first floor; Uncle Lando and Victor had accommodation somewhere at the top of the house; we didn't see much of Mr. Constantine but the library was regarded as a possible place to find him; and when I wasn't with Granny I had my comfortable bed-sitting-room. We all came together for lunch and dinner except when Uncle Lando was 'not feeling too good today', as Aunt Ada put it, which meant he was being sillier than usual and not fit to sit at table; and except when Mr. Constantine was 'too busy at the mill' to come back for a meal. For some days I believed the Treworgey Mill was producing cloth or wool — some of the wool Granny and I consumed with our knitting needles perhaps — but 'the mill' proved to be a saw-mill and that accounted for the whining of machinery noise that could be heard in the distance when the wind was blowing from the south. Part of the Treworgey estate was now planted with pines and other useful building-wood trees, and these, after felling, were sawn to plank lengths at the mill and then sent off along the 'new' road to Treluz Major on the way to Plymouth. Pit props and fencing posts were also prepared here, and sections for the construction of 'The Constantine' put-it-up-yourself garden shed that I'd seen advertised.

Although women came from the village to do the heaviest housework there were no permanent indoor servants — Mimsy was not regarded as a servant — and no one to wait on us at meal times. Aunt Ada sat at the top of the long table with a pile of plates in front of her and she apportioned the main dish and we passed the plates to each other; we served ourselves with vegetables. Mimsy's dishes were of the old-fashioned kind: she brought in such things as large cottage pies, the fluffy potato tops of which were golden brown, never burnt; or mutton broth made without any fat meat — Mr. Constantine objected to a creamy soup so we ladled cream into this ourselves; it was delicious. Our cream, milk, butter and eggs were sent over from the farm and were always perfect for quality and freshness — the farm was another part of the Treworgey estate though it was a long time before I discovered its exact location.

Uncle Lando could talk fairly sensibly at times though I was nervous of getting too involved in speech with him, feeling I might touch on subjects beyond his comprehension. He had a disconcerting habit of starting conversations in what seemed to be their middle: he would say, 'Yes, I agree with you, Edward,' though Mr. Constantine hadn't spoken, or, 'I wanted you to do that, Aunt Ada,' though Aunt Ada had done nothing unusual. Perhaps there were wise thoughts in his poor head; profound judgements struggling to get out; and these odd detached sentences were all he could voice. Mr. Constantine, coming last to the table and being the first to leave, would pat his shoulder and Uncle Lando would smile happily up at him; they were all kind to the simpleton though Granny, I think, preferred to forget his existence; to forget that once he had been her beloved younger son: Edward's — Mr. Constantine's — father had been older and the heir to the estate.

3

I enjoyed life at Treworgey: my room was comfortable; the bathroom on my landing seemed never to be used by anyone but me and there was always plenty of hot water; the food was nicer than I'd ever had; and although it had been easy enough to get out into the countryside from Plymouth and the sea was close at hand, here we were totally surrounded by garden and fields and woods and I believed the sea was near though it wasn't in view from the house. It was a lovely place!

As the days went by I learnt that Granny kept her own rooms clean and tidy, that she read at least one romantic novel each week — her eyesight was remarkably good, though for reading she used a mother-of-pearl-framed magnifying-glass, moving it along the lines as she read — and, of course, she had her knitting. She liked to walk in the garden, to go to church — St. Cuthberts — on Sundays, and to visit the churchyard most afternoons. After the wet day of my arrival we had perfect summer weather and Granny and I would stroll down the lane to the church and after resting a while on the stone-slab seats in the porch we would wander amongst the graves. Granny greeted each one as a friend — it was her only old-age peculiarity. She would read the inscriptions on the headstones — well known to her and soon well known to me — pat the stones, say 'Hello' and 'Good-bye'. She told me all about the dead people, their virtues and vices, characteristics and capabilities, speaking as if they were still living — but I took it this wasn't the sort of thing I was meant to make notes of. The family graves naturally had most attention, and one of these was that of Mr. Edward Constantine's father — her elder son — and his wife who were buried together in a corner plot: he had died of wounds received at Dunkirk and she had taken an overdose of tablets soon afterwards — 'Wanted to keep him company, I suppose,' remarked Granny sympathetically. Their son, Mr. Edward, had been brought up jointly — and, I guessed, quarrelsomely — by Granny and Aunt Ada, for when Aunt Ada married she and her husband had lived at Treworgey. Now Mr. Edward was head of the family. There was another grave she gave particular attention to: a man and his wife named Northey were buried here, but these she never talked about; I didn't know who they were and felt I shouldn't ask questions.

We would take the whole afternoon on these expeditions and somehow it didn't seem a morbid occupation. Granny walked with a stick in one hand, her other hand holding my arm; the sunshine poured down on us but she liked hot weather and wore a wide-brimmed, rose-trimmed straw hat to protect her face; despite her age and slowness she gave the impression that she was on her way to Ascot. In the house she kept to her own rooms most of the day and barred Aunt Ada from entry whenever possible. She was a sweet, kind, strong-willed old lady with firm views on current affairs; she kept up-to-date through newspapers and her radio. With the exception of her grandson, Mr. Edward, she had a poor opinion of the occupants of Treworgey, and a poor opinion of its management: the place wasn't like it used to be, too much was changed; whatever was the world coming to!

She and I got on well together; I enjoyed her company and she seemed to like me; there was only one snag: I wasn't doing the job I was engaged to do. I'd made no notes, done no typing, for except for the tales in the churchyard Granny had been uncommunicative. She talked, but not about old times; she questioned me about myself, about the other jobs I'd had, about Plymouth; and we discussed the day-by-day news; but we weren't making any progress regarding her memories of the past. I tried to lead her into reminiscence but to no avail; perhaps she was intentionally reticent because she wanted to keep me there longer for companionship — I suppose she was aware of the purpose of my presence — or perhaps just at this time, and because I was there and she had new things to think of, her memory was fading — though for her graveyard friends it was as bright as ever.

At Mr. Edward's request — it was impossible to think of him as Mr. Constantine when they all called him Edward — I'd stayed on at Treworgey when the expected fortnight's stay had elapsed, but when I'd been there a month, receiving a breakfast-plate cheque at the end of each week, I began to feel guilty. No one questioned me, asked how much I'd written or if the note-taking was going well, and I decided I must do something about it: I would speak to Mr. Edward; explain. So one morning, knowing him to be in the library, I went to the little sitting-room meaning to go through and tell him how impossible my task was proving to be. Aunt Ada was hoovering the sitting-room carpet and was surprised to see me. She switched off the noise and I said: 'I'm going to the library; I want to speak to Mr. Edward,' and she replied, 'Oh, I shouldn't do that, dear.'

'Why not?' I asked.

'He doesn't like to be disturbed. There are strict orders that no one must bother him, and we all obey.'

There was that word 'obey' again. Tom Pacey had used it at the railway station the evening of my arrival and it had seemed the wrong word then; it was even more strange from an aunt regarding her nephew. Although at our first meeting I'd thought Mr. Edward kind and friendly I hadn't had much contact with him since except at meal times when he appeared to be a silent, taciturn man, kind to Uncle Lando but merely enduring the rest of us. I hadn't been able to make up my mind about him: apparently he was an overbearing brute of a man! I was exasperated with Aunt Ada's mildness! It was likely I'd be leaving Treworgey now so I didn't care what I said. 'Why does he have to be obeyed?' I asked sharply. 'Who does he think he is — God?'

Aunt Ada looked hurt and for her sake I regretted what I'd said and was going to abandon my visit to Mr. Edward, but we were both startled to hear his voice saying, 'Ask Miss Kingsley to come into the library, Aunt Ada,' and there he was at the open door of that room and had probably heard my remarks about him. He spoke to his aunt, ignoring me, but this could have been to emphasize to her that I had permission to enter his so-private place, the library.

He held the door open for me then shut it behind us, giving the impression he was locking it, then said: 'Please sit down, Miss Kingsley.' I sat in the chair opposite his desk, feeling like a schoolchild called to the headmaster's study to answer for wrongdoing. I felt I shouldn't have tried to get into the library to see him. He sat on the edge of the desk and, looking not at me but out of the window, said: 'You think me an ogre, so let me explain why I make such a strict rule about not being disturbed when I'm here. This is the only place where I can do the accounts, write letters and such, in peace; I also bring the paper-work concerning the mill here for attention, it's too noisy to do it down there. Aunt Ada, bless her, does well with the housekeeping really, but she's a worrier and if I didn't keep this room out-of-bounds to her she would be coming in every few minutes or so expecting me to solve her problems; as it is she breaks the rules sometimes, unconsciously perhaps. And Miss Mimms would probably be coming in to tell me the beans were burning — she and Aunt Ada were at boarding-school together, you know, and in spite of the fact that my aunt married they've managed to practically hold hands ever since. Aunt Ada, living a sheltered life here as the daughter of the house and then, later, with her husband to turn to, never had to make decisions, there was always someone to do that for her; and Miss Mimms, although a splendid cook, is rather woolly-minded: I *have* to keep them at arm's length! I have so many responsibilities: besides their welfare there's Uncle Lando and Victor, Granny and yourself, the staff, the estate, the farm and the mill all needing my attention; plus my commitments in the village where I'm a landlord to some and a kind of squire, and also some involvement with the affairs of Treluz Minor and even Treluz Major. Do you begrudge me one small space on this earth where I can be alone and quiet and give my attention to questions that concern us all!'

I was frightened; I hadn't meant to provoke him. 'Oh no,' I assured him. 'I'm sorry; I didn't mean to bother you.' I stood up to leave.

He stood up too and pulled forward the chintz-covered easy chair. 'Forgive my outburst,' he said. 'Sit here instead and tell me what it was you wanted.'

I'd nearly forgotten what I'd come for. I cleared my mind of the jumble of worries — his worries — that had clouded it while he talked. 'It's about Granny,' I told him. 'I think I'd better give up; I'm not making any progress with the stories you wanted recorded.'

'You get on all right together, don't you? She's happy, she likes you.'

'Oh, I like her too, but she's not talking about the past; she talks about me and my concerns.'

'Do you mind that?'

'No, not at all, I've no secrets; but it's not what I'm here for, is it? I'm being paid for doing nothing.'

'I shouldn't worry about that. Wait and see what happens. Perhaps suddenly she'll start talking about old times again. Anyway, you mustn't complicate my life even more by leaving us now.' He said this laughingly, referring to his earlier tirade; then he surprised me by asking, 'Are you happy here? Do you like Treworgey?'

'It's perfect!' I exclaimed. 'I love it!'

'I love Treworgey too, though I sometimes feel guilty for being the owner.'

'Guilty? Why?'

'Well, Aunt Ada loves it too, and so would Uncle Lando if he was normal — if he hadn't been thrown from his pony when he was a boy and had to exchange intelligence for imbecility and a desire to overeat; yet because I'm the son of their elder brother the place is mine. And Granny must remember how things were when she was mistress here, and it must have seemed to belong to her then. It's hardly fair, for they knew Treworgey at its best, when there was no commercialism, no saw-mills — that's due to me, the estate couldn't have been kept going without some money-making background. They all have a share in the mill; we formed a Company; but the house and farm and everything else belongs to me — and the responsibilities that go with it!

I didn't know what to say. The white dog — Jasper — which had been dozing on the hearthrug came to me and put a paw on my knee as if, like his master, needing sympathy, though I wasn't very concerned for Mr. Edward for I felt he was well able to cope and had merely been letting off steam. I patted Jasper's head: 'Shall I take him for a walk?' I asked, thinking perhaps that would be helpful, but Mr. Edward replied, 'I'm afraid he's a one-man dog; in any case he doesn't need much exercise, he's quite old, you know. Granny gave him to me as a puppy on one of my birthdays — it must be fourteen or fifteen years ago now. Dear Granny! Stay with us, Miss Kingsley, and keep her company, keep her happy, and I'll be very grateful to you.'

So I remained at Treworgey for another month enjoying the easy-life existence of knitting and strolls to the churchyard; then one morning when

Aunt Ada took Granny her early cup of tea she couldn't wake her; she came for me because my room was nearest and I went back with her and together we realised that the old lady was dead: in her sleep she had dreamed her way into the the land of her churchyard relations and friends. I was glad she slipped away so peacefully: at ninety she couldn't have had long to live and as she grew weaker would have hated inactivity, perhaps even being unable to knit; would have hated to depend on others for everything.

I went to the funeral with the family, grieving as they were grieving; as we stood at the graveside after the ceremony I was sorry I'd not been able to record Granny's memories: her knowledge of the locality; the events, important and unimportant, that she'd remembered were lost for ever now, as the soft-winged, brilliant butterflies that fluttered amongst the funeral flowers would soon be gone too. An infinite sadness at the impermanence, the vulnerability of mankind flooded my mind: a lifetime was very little when one thought of time as a whole; we were soon gone and most of us would soon be forgotten.

4

Now my stay at Treworgey was ended; there was no excuse to remain longer. That night I did my packing and in the morning after breakfast I asked Aunt Ada if, later that day, Tom Pacey might drive me to the station for the early-evening train. I could say my good-byes at lunch-time, our last meal together, and I hoped I wouldn't embarrass them by weeping, for besides missing poor Granny I knew I was going to miss them all very much. To my surprise Aunt Ada was very upset at my request. She said: 'Granny's gone and Edward has driven off to London on business; if you go too there will be no one left! And you can't possibly leave without saying goodbye to Edward; I know he'll be terribly cross if I let you go before he comes back!'

So, not unwillingly of course, I

unpacked and stayed there, trying to find things to do, to help, to pay for my keep. Mr. Edward was away for three weeks, part of which time the mill was closed for Bank Holiday and the following annual works' holiday. I finished Granny's last piece of knitting and packed her last parcel for Oxfam; I helped a bit in the kitchen and settled one or two difficulties that arose — Mr. Edward was right, Aunt Ada and Mimsy were inclined to panic if things went wrong — and I made friends with Uncle Lando.

Victor, who was rather a moody young man, complained that he had no free time so I suggested he have some days off while I looked after Uncle Lando. If Mr. Edward had been at home perhaps Victor would have been afraid to accept my offer, but with our employer away he agreed to let me take on his work and several times went off to Plymouth for the day, returning by the late train — he had a bicycle for transport to and from the railway station. Meanwhile I spent the time with Uncle Lando whose top, barred-window rooms had once been the nursery.

Luckily, he was always in a fairly sensible state when I was in charge and we got on well with each other. A lot of his time was spent in putting together large jigsaw puzzles and, more easily seeing the correct sections, I would guide his podgy fingers to the right spot and he would thump the piece into place with a delighted smile on his poor foolish face. Some of the jigsaw pictures that were spread on the long nursery table were put together quite wrongly with ill-fitting pieces forced into position, giving weird, surrealistic effects. We also played childish games — ludo, snakes-and-ladders and tiddly-winks; Uncle Lando kept to no rules and always believed he'd won the game: it didn't matter, he was happy.

I tried to discover the extent of his intelligence, or lack of it, and gave him little word-card-choosing tests or poem lines to repeat: sometimes he was clever but mostly nothing stayed in his mind for longer than a minute or two. I also ministered to his physical needs by helping him on and off with his jacket — an exercise he felt was necessary quite often — by changing his shoes which he also liked to do a lot, and by combing his silky brown hair. I even cut his hair one afternoon: I gave him a mirror and stood behind him while I trimmed the stray strands of his — as it looked to me — pudding-basin haircut. His small eyes, deep in flabby flesh, watched every move I made; he grinned back at me through the mirror; I made a funny face at him and he doubled up with laughter, nearly dropping the mirror. When I'd finished the job and removed the towel from his shoulders he caught my hand and kissed it, becoming for a moment a courtly gentleman of another period. I ruffled his hair in reply, spoiling my handiwork, and had to use the comb again.

I found him a lovable chap, but I was

only doing part-time duty: I could see that Victor had a taxing and perhaps, long-term, boring task in looking after him; and I hadn't seen him in one of his tantrums or silliest moods when, I'd been told, he behaved like a fretful infant, throwing his possessions round the room or refusing to move from his chair even to go to the toilet, making Victor wait on him hand and foot. But pity was bound to be uppermost in my feelings for Uncle Lando.

During these weeks I made friends with Jasper, too, who was moping for his master. I took him for walks, but not far from the house, just through the garden as far as the pond which was fed by the stream flowing down from the woods; it was sun-warmed and secluded there and had been a favourite spot for Granny and me. Jasper was unhappy if too long away from the house and preferred to lie in the hall, in awkward places where he might be stumbled over, listening for Mr. Edward's return.

Granny, of course, hadn't been able to walk far and except for our strolls in the garden and to the churchyard I'd seen nothing of the estate; now I explored farther, following paths through the woods wondering where they would lead me. One afternoon I came to a clearing where trees — pine trees, I thought they were — had recently been felled. It was fairly high ground, a hillside, and I found I was looking down on the saw-mill, silent now during the holiday or I would have known where I was heading. I sat on the dry sandy soil and studied the mill: a yard with stacks of logs and sawn planks and piles of sawdust and shavings; various tin-roofed sheds; a small, glass-windowed building that might be an office; and parked lorries on an asphalt area near the road that led back to Treluz Major. Deep in the valley, the mill and its activities were hidden from Treworgey; even the road — Granny's new road in her memories of fifty or sixty years ago — didn't run close to the house: if all this land belonged to the Constantines they'd been able to plan it that way to preserve their privacy.

To my surprise water — the sea — filled the valley below the mill and I realised this must be Hawken Creek — Granny had remembered the days when sailing boats came up at high tide. The water was dark green and calm, with no waves so far inland as this though perhaps there were waves in winter time or in rough weather. Trees grew right down to the water's edge both sides of the creek; the oak trees, with bending boughs dipping in the water, were like old women washing linen in some foreign sea; points of sunlight glittering through the leaves were reflected and gave the effect of a dot-and-dash impressionist painting. A rowing boat was tied up to the small jetty: it was a queer shape, almost the shape of a pear. There was a lyrical quality about the scene; I felt the boat was waiting there for someone — perhaps me — to float away down river to a land of wondrous beauty, a land beyond the boundaries of this small earth we lived in. I was probably still under the spell of Tennyson's 'Morte d'Arthur' which I'd been reading to Uncle Lando that morning — he hadn't understood the poem but had enjoyed the words and rhythm I thought, at any rate he'd sat contentedly still while I read.

It was lovely resting there high above the mill in complete silence except for the twittering of birds; then I heard footsteps, someone was marching briskly along the road below: it was Tom Pacey and he had a carrier bag in one hand and an old-fashioned billy-can in the other. I didn't want to climb down to the road and there was no need to make my presence known to him; unless he looked upwards and had the eyes of a hawk he wouldn't spot me, my brown jacket was the colour of the earth around. I watched as he went into the yard and opened his bag; I couldn't think what he was up to; then from various lairs and hide-outs came cats — I counted seven; tabbies and tortoiseshells — and Tom fed them scraps he'd brought and poured milk from the can into a saucer. These must be saw-mill cats, cats to keep down mice and rats, and probably they were normally fed from the workmen's lunch packets, and Tom, knowing they would be having a thin time during the holidays, had come from the village to succour them. I liked Tom. He was the old type of servant; devoted, loyal, and happy to spend his life working for the Constantines; his wife, too, had worked for the family till recently when she became too ill to manage more than her own household chores. I liked Tom even more now; I was fond of cats myself though there were none at the house because Aunt Ada didn't like them; I was pleased that these were being looked after.

When Tom had gone home I turned back through the woods to Treworgey: the saw-mill was no longer merely a sound, it was real to me now.

Mr. Edward came home that evening, putting in an appearance at dinner-time and surprising me though Aunt Ada must have known the day of his return; she may have thought I was aware of it too, she was inclined to presume I knew more of the affairs of Treworgey than I actually did. Mimsy, too, must have expected him for she produced a splendid meal; and Mr. Edward opened a bottle of wine. It was almost as if we were having a celebration but really I think it was that we'd mourned for Granny these last weeks and this seemed the moment to be happy again. As we left the table I asked Mr. Edward if I could have a word with him next morning and he agreed straight away, saying, 'Yes, how about eleven o'clock in the library?' as if he, too, knew it was time I thought of leaving, which rather disappointed me and I hoped Aunt Ada had been right in persuading me to stay till now; perhaps he'd been surprised to find me still there.

When I went to the library in the

morning I found the door welcomingly open and as soon as Jasper and I had greeted each other and Mr. Edward had led me to the comfortable chair Aunt Ada came in carrying a tray with coffee and biscuits. Smiling at me she put down the tray and left us, carefully shutting the door. I decided they were softening the blow, as it were; though I had no right to expect anything but dismissal now, I'd had an easy, luxurious time at Treworgey — with payment too!

Mr. Edward didn't sit down but stood at the window looking out at the masses of late summer flowers, roses and phlox and ragged sun-daisies, that crowded the overgrown garden — overgrown because Tom Pacey, being chauffeur and odd-jobs man too, had little time left to keep it in order. The silence was becoming awkward to me so, sipping my coffee and trying to be business-like, I said: 'I've been very happy here; thank you for letting me stay so long. Can Mr. Pacey run me to the station this afternoon or, if that's not convenient, for one of tomorrow's trains?'

He turned and looked at me then, and I gazed back at him, at his kind and thoughtful face that I knew could twist in anger and irritation sometimes. He said: 'Why are you always in such a hurry to get back to Plymouth? Granny told me once that you've no relations or proper home.'

'No, I'm practically alone in the world,' I agreed. 'I shared a flat with another girl but I gave that up when I found I was staying here longer than a month, it seemed silly to pay the rent and not be there. But there's nothing for me to do here now Granny's gone.'

'There's plenty for you to do — and you *have* been doing plenty according to Aunt Ada. She's told me how you've tended Uncle Lando, how you've helped in the various 'crises' she's so good at creating; and you're the only female Jasper has ever taken notice of, you've been a comfort to him.' He stared out at the flowers again and I wondered what he was thinking: was he going to ask me to stay and be a sort of general help? I looked at Jasper lying on the rug and fancied he winked at me, as if he were saying, 'I've given you good recommendation.' Then Mr. Edward turned and said casually, as though remarking on the weather, 'I think it would be a good idea if you and I were to marry. Now don't look so startled, it's not so bad as it sounds. Treworgey needs a mistress. As my wife you could take control without upsetting Aunt Ada and Miss Mimms, they would welcome someone they can turn to in emergencies, someone to accept responsibility. You would take that load off my shoulders; and you could keep an eye on Uncle Lando — I'm not quite satisfied with Victor, though he seems to do his job well enough; you could help me with the accounts — take them over altogether perhaps — and type letters and all sorts of things like that.' He was calmly listing chores for me as if he'd memorised them, and I sat there struck dumb, not believing my ears! Was I dreaming this? Finally, after a long pause, Mr. Edward came to what must have been the main point of the matter to us both; he said: 'When I said it would not be as bad as it sounds I meant I would expect no physical — sexual — response from you. You could take your time about that, I'd not bother you till you were ready for me.'

I still couldn't speak — or move; I felt screwed to the chair; and now that he was touching on the natural reasons for marriage — love-making — my face flamed red. I'd never thought myself to be attractive to men, I believed no man had ever looked twice at me. I was nearly thirty years old and considered myself an old maid. I had nice, almost black hair but no rosy cheeks and blue eyes to go with it but a pale skin and brown eyes; and I was thin with bony arms and legs and a practically non-existent bust; nor was I a sparkling, witty talker, I dried up if men tried to make conversation with me. I knew no man would want me and thought Mr. Edward was only mentioning the sex side of marriage from a conventional point of view, or not to hurt my feelings; or perhaps he thought I'd want children. After all, if I'd been sexy and he desired me he would have made his proposal from that angle instead of being carefully, coldly explanatory. But now as he turned from the window and came towards me he was suddenly frighteningly male. I felt like screaming and running from the library to hide in my room, but instead I heard myself saying: 'If you don't drink your coffee it will be cold.'

He burst into laughter and that helped me. 'You sound just like a wife already, saying that,' he teased. Then he continued seriously, '*Will* you marry me, Catherine? Let's get married first and do our courting later on when we have time for it.'

When we had time for it! Although I knew little of love and marriage I was sure lovers didn't wait till there was time to caress and kiss; their bodily desires sent them into each other's arms at every opportunity. For some reason — the ones he'd quoted, I suppose — Mr. Edward wanted a wife; I was conveniently close at hand. 'Why can't I just stay and do the things you suggest without us being married?' I asked, coming to life a little now as I assessed the circumstances.

'It wouldn't be the same. You need the authority to back you, to stop Aunt Ada saying, 'Yes, I believe you're right but I must ask Edward first'. Besides, she and the various 'gentry' round here have been trying to find a partner for me for ages: I prefer to make my own arrangements and shall enjoy presenting them with a 'fait accompli'.'

Obviously he was only suggesting marriage to suit himself — and a cold, queer marriage it would be! But why shouldn't I take advantage of his offer I would pull my weight; do all he asked and more: they were wasteful in th kitchen and I might, diplomatically, save him money there; I could take over some of the gardening to help Tom Pacey; and of course I would help with Uncle Lando in any way I could, and be a kind of secretary to Mr. Edward himself. I stood up, feeling surprisingly in command of the situation, and said calmly, 'I'll think about it'; and as he still hadn't touched his coffee I carried the tray back to the kitchen leaving him to close the door after me without having had acceptance or refusal from me.

But there was no doubt what my answer would be: most people would condemn me for accepting marriage on these terms, but no girl who'd been as poor as I had all my life, or as lonely, or of so little account, would turn down the chance to be mistress of Treworgey. I even wished — crazily and momen-tarily — that Mr. Edward had said he loved me: I didn't love him but would have paid with my body as well as in all other ways for the honour he was doing me. I didn't have much confidence, wasn't the kind of person to hand out orders — I was glad the domestic pattern of Treworgey was already established, I wouldn't really have to be boss to anyone — but I intended to give enthusiastic help to everyone and deserve my position in the family. I felt dedicated. I thought of the churchyard, full of long-ago Constantines: I was to be one of them; when I died let the inscription on my gravestone be, 'She came with nothing but departed in possession of us all'! Aunt Ada should be my mother, Uncle Lando my child, and Mr. Edward my father, brother — and husband. And Mimsy, tiny Mimsy who flittered about the kitchen like an anxious, hard-working mouse, should be my conscience, keeping me up to the mark.

Mr. Edward didn't come to the table at lunch-time and Aunt Ada accounted for this, saying he was gone to the mill where there was a lot to attend to after his absence. I fancied she looked at me questioningly and wondered if she knew of her nephew's proposal to me, but decided she was just naturally curious to know what had taken place between us in the library and whether I was to leave Treworgey now. Watching her carve the chicken and fill our plates I realised she was virtually mistress here herself and had been for years: despite what Mr. Edward had said, she might be very put out by a usurper — myself — and I would do well to find out how she felt about it before I took her place; my further happiness at Treworgey depended very much on her.

So after lunch when she and Mimsy and myself were having a cup of tea in the little sitting-room — the menfolk of the house weren't tea drinkers, at least not at lunch-time — I began to hope that Mimsy would leave Aunt Ada and me alone for a while as she sometimes did when eager to get on with the washing-up or to bake a cake for tea. I knew Mimsy would be no problem to me for she was Aunt Ada's shadow in deed and thought regarding the family and Treworgey, but I felt her presence was superfluous for the telling of my news. She *did* finish her tea before us — we were having a second cup — and as soon as she'd departed I turned to Aunt Ada and, thinking it best not to prevaricate, said: 'Mr. Edward has asked me to marry him. I was so astonished I haven't given him an answer yet. How do you feel about it, Aunt Ada?'

I couldn't tell if I'd surprised her or not but certainly she was delighted with the idea and showed no dismay or jealousy that I would be mistress of the house if I married her nephew; perhaps it was born and bred in her that the male line inherits and their wives take precedence over daughters and sisters and aunts; at any rate she leant across and kissed me, taking it for granted I was going to accept the proposal, and replied, 'Nothing could please me better, my dear. I've come to love you as I would a daughter — I wish I'd had a daughter instead of a son. You won't find me obstructive, Catherine, and Treworgey needs a proper mistress, someone young like you; you will have children and start the family line again and that will be a tonic to us all.'

I was aware that she had a son but believed him to be something of a black sheep and best not brought into conversation. He'd moved away from the district and wasn't going to complicate things for me. At the moment he was regarded as Mr. Edward's heir — poor Uncle Lando didn't count, I suppose — and he was likely to remain so during the platonic marriage between his cousin and myself; but Mr. Edward and I had our lives to live first, I needn't think in terms of inheritance, and in the years to come if it happened that my husband died first and I was left a widow I would move away from Treworgey, not stay and watch it change or decline under other hands as Granny had done.

My thinking of the future in this way

proved to me that I was going to say 'Yes' to Mr. Edward and I made myself omit the 'Mr.' from then on. I wondered if I would ever come to call my husband 'Ted' or 'Teddy' and smiled: it was so unlikely, and pet names didn't suit him. Aunt Ada, pouring herself a third cup of tea, said, 'There, you look happy now; I was beginning to wonder if something I'd said had upset you. Why don't you go for a walk in the garden and plan your trousseau and the wedding; and we must think about putting the best bedroom ready: Edward is sleeping in one of the top rooms that used to be for servants — like a monk, he is; I've always thought it wrong for a man to live like that!'

I hurriedly escaped to the garden. Trousseaus and weddings and best bedrooms were things I hadn't considered yet and somehow hadn't expected to be involved with. I strolled between the high privet hedges to the pond. Wild-growing michaelmas daisies, shading from near-white to deep purple, crowded the borders here, smothering less sturdy plants; it was nearly October now but still warm. Tall clumps of pampas-grass grew round the path that circled the pond and I didn't see Edward, who was sitting on the wrought-iron half-circle garden seat where Granny and I used to rest, till I was close to him — he wasn't at the mill as Aunt Ada had believed. I hoped he didn't think I'd sought him out; yet what did it matter if he did? I had to give him my answer sometime, why not now?

He made a place for me on the seat, saying, 'Come, Catherine, sit down; I'm feeling restless, mentally I mean, and haven't got back to my working routine yet. I'm letting the mill look after itself for once.' He was in a gentle mood and I forgot he could be otherwise: sharp and impatient.

We sat together, talking about ordinary day-to-day happenings while Jasper, who was stretched out in the sunshine beside us, puffed doggy snoring noises into the still air. I began to wonder if I'd dreamt Edward's proposal or if he'd had second thoughts about it, but I was more at ease with him than at any time previously; I generally felt ignorant and tongue-tied in his presence for his long face and serious expression gave him a look of wisdom and strength. I turned to gaze at him: I'd had no brothers — or sisters — and I thought again that he would be more like a brother to me than a husband, or like the father I couldn't remember. He smiled. 'How about it, then? Will you marry me?' he asked casually, making the matter seem unimportant; and I replied as lightly as I could. 'The answer is 'yes', if you think it will work out all right.'

We stood up and for an awful moment I thought he was going to kiss me, but instead we shook hands as if at the conclusion of a business arrangement, which in a way was what our marriage would be. Then we walked back to the house together and told Aunt Ada our news — which was no news to her for she'd assumed my acceptance. Her pleasure though, expressed now to Edward as well as to me, made me feel I'd done the right thing.

5

So Edward and I were married: not married, as Aunt Ada would have liked, at the near-by St. Cuthberts with bells and bridesmaids and a crowded congregation but at the Registry Office in Treluz Major with only herself and Mimsy as witnesses. Aunt Ada had plans for our wedding, I'd discovered. 'You will look lovely in white satin,' she told me, 'and with your dark hair and pale complexion I think your bouquet should be pink roses; and pink or perhaps crimson for your going-away outfit.' When she learnt there would be no white wedding, even no honeymoon, she was shocked; I think she felt that without them we would not be properly married; but when Edward had convinced her with excuses that as the wedding was to be as soon as could be arranged there was no time for fripperies, as he called it, and that he was too busy at the mill for a honeymoon, she said, coyly, 'Well, I don't suppose it matters to couples in love where they spend the first night.'

She prepared the big bedroom for us, calling it the master bedroom, which luckily was connected with a large dressing-room that either Edward or I could use for sleeping, there was a bed there. From the beginning we'd agreed that Aunt Ada should think our marriage was a proper one for she would never have understood or condoned our 'marriage of convenience'. Edward came down from his attic and I moved up a floor; it was the floor where Aunt Ada and Mimsy had rooms and I think we might have had difficulty in keeping our strange behaviour a secret from them but Aunt Ada decided to move down to Granny's room and for Mimsy to have my former room so that left Edward and I with a floor to ourselves.

Throughout the ceremony at the Registry Office Aunt Ada wept into an inadequate lace-edged handkerchief, playing the role of reluctant mother to us both — reluctant to lose her off-spring; but back at the house she was happy and excited. There was no real wedding reception but we had Tom Pacey and his wife, and a few other villagers connected with Treworgey or the mill, in for the cutting of the beautiful wedding cake baked and decorated by Mimsy, and glasses of celebration champagne. Uncle Lando and Victor didn't join us: I suppose Uncle Lando had always been kept out of sight to some extent — there was still some feeling of shame regarding mental illness — or perhaps Aunt Ada had thought his wolfing of cake or the effect intoxicating drink would have on him would spoil things for us — I would have liked to have seen him there.

Later Aunt Ada decreed that Edward and I must dine alone in the little sitting-room — the party had been held in the seldom-used big drawing-room. Edward opened more champagne with our meal and I became quite tipsy, inclined to giggle, nearer to being drunk than I'd ever been. It helped to make the situation less odd and perhaps Edward was encouraging me to drink for this reason. We went to bed early, Edward helping me upstairs because my legs seemed filled with bubbles, and we must have appeared appropriately new-married, lover-like enough to please Aunt Ada; I was certain she was peepingly watching us from her room, not with curiosity but satisfaction. We entered our new bedroom together and Edward locked the door. He led me to the bed and I sat down to regain my senses; he crossed to the dressing-room which was to be his bedroom. I don't know if he locked that between-door, I didn't dare try the handle; in fact it was months before I knew if it was locked at night for Edward always rose early and passed through my room while I was still asleep. It was disturbing to think he saw me sleeping: some mornings I woke early myself and tried to keep awake to hear him go through, but it was like waiting for Father Christmas on Christmas Eve — one never quite managed it.

Now that it was autumn I spent the evenings in the little sitting-room with Aunt Ada and Mimsy. Sometimes Edward joined us for an hour, but always he came to collect me at bedtime. He would say: 'Come, Catherine, time for bed,' and even romantic Aunt Ada must have been convinced he was an eager husband. I made it one of my chores to keep our rooms clean and tidy, to change the bed linen, so she was unaware that we were using two beds; our dirty laundry was sent to Treluz Minor for washing and I took over the listing and checking so there was no reason for her to wonder why we were using too many sheets. I think as time went by I might have relaxed my care to keep her in the dark but was afraid that if she discovered our peculiar arrangements she would do her best to bring us closer together and cause a lot of embarrassment.

It was strange how contented I was those first weeks; anyone would have thought I *was* happily married, in a proper way. I kept my resolution to work hard and give good value but although Aunt Ada tried to take second place, to defer to me — she consulted me on each day's menu and the working routine for the cleaning women — it was obvious that the domestic affairs of Treworgey were already in competent hands, though she did, it's true, lose her head sometimes. I was able to settle some problems: to persuade the electrician to come over from Treluz Major and attend to a faulty switch — Aunt Ada had phoned him repeatedly about this with no effect — and things like that. I'd never considered myself a capable person, but because Edward believed in me I found I *could* make decisions and take charge when necessary. Aunt Ada and Mimsy had faith in my efficiency too, so I *was* efficient.

I told Edward that I thought Victor

should have a fixed day off every week instead of odd times that depended on when Tom Pacey was free to take charge of Uncle Lando, and when he agreed to this I looked after Uncle Lando myself; he'd grown fond of me and was always at his best those days. And I did some gardening which at this time of year was confined to clipping and clearing and bonfire burning.

I think I was most useful with the book-keeping; both household and mill book-keeping. I offered to go to the mill but Edward refused to let me, saying that the building I'd taken to be an office was where the loads were checked out and that the joking and swearing that went on there wasn't fit for my ears; so I worked alone in the library nearly every morning, struggling with his complicated system which doubled the paper-work. He had no office-work help at the mill, dealt with all the accounts himself, and as I sorted and simplified Costs, Sales, Wages, P.A.Y.E. and Taxation I understood why he'd excluded Aunt Ada from the library; she must have been the last straw to him sometimes! He was a working boss when at the mill too, I could tell that by the state of his clothes; he also had to keep an eye on the farm, on the estate, and on the house itself and its occupants. He *did* have too much to do and I was pleased to be able to relieve him of some of the pressures. He seemed happier now, more relaxed; he whistled sometimes and although the tunes were unrecognisable they were jolly ones; he teased Aunt Ada and praised Mimsy's cooking — he hadn't done this before — and he was even more patient with Uncle Lando.

Edward had presented me with a bank book bearing my new name — Mrs. Catherine Constantine — and a cheque book; every quarter he was going to pay in what he called my dress allowance and it was to be my money to do what I liked with. The amount was more than my earnings had been when

I had to keep myself; with everything as plentiful as it was at Treworgey I needed less cash than ever before and I'd never been extravagant, rent had always been my worst expense; but when I protested that this allowance was unnecessary he took no notice and wouldn't discuss the matter.

I decided that the best thing to do was to use the money for clothes; Edward had called it a dress allowance, perhaps he thought me dowdy. I'd worn my best coat for the wedding but it was by no means new: now I would try to dress to match my position. So Tom Pacey drove me over to Treluz Major in the Bentley and I did some shopping. The ultra-fashionable styles didn't suit me nor did I think them right for Treworgey, so I bought a couple of good tweed outfits and some frilly-necked blouses to make them less homely, and a pair of strong walking shoes. When I got home I gave Aunt Ada and Mimsy a fashion parade in the little sitting-room and they were pleased with my purchases. 'You've got good taste, dear,' said Aunt Ada; and Mimsy added, 'How lovely to be young and able to wear such nice things; our fashions in the twenties and thirties were so ugly, or so it seems to me now.' I glanced sympathetically at Mimsy: besides being as quiet as a mouse, not talking much — but always busy — she was also mouselike in appearance; she kept to grey and mauve for her dresses, and although she scurried about the house in quite good, fairly high-heeled shoes, sometimes when I thought of her I saw her as in button boots, sprigged muslin and a bonnet — she was the 'Mrs. Mouse' of one of my childhood picture books. Aunt Ada, too, wore 'sensible' clothes but she liked hard, bright colours that didn't suit her. But they were pleased with my new clothes and I hoped that in this case their judgement was good.

One of my new outfits was a pink tweed skirt with a waistcoat, not a jacket, and I was wearing this and a white, lacy Victorian-style blouse with a cheeky pink velvet bow at the neck one Sunday afternoon when I went for a walk. We went to church Sunday mornings, had a rather late lunch, then Aunt Ada and Mimsy generally indulged in a nap, dozing in their chairs in the little sitting-room; I didn't know what Edward did on Sunday afternoons. It was November but the weather was lovely, warm and sunny, a day belonging to summer except that golden leaves were floating down from the oak trees as I walked through the woods and wispy oldman's beard enveloped the bramble bushes growing beside the path; briony, too, clung in vivid red clusters amongst the few remaining blackberries. The berries were thick this year and Tom Pacey had warned me to expect a hard winter: 'Nature supplies the birds with plenty of berries when bad weather's to come,' he'd said — he was a close-to-the-earth man and although he now drove the Bentley he had formerly worked with horses; he loved and respected all animals and birds.

Thinking of Tom, I remembered the day I'd seen him at the mill and decided to walk that way; it was Sunday, no one would be there. When I came to the clearing and gazed down on Hawken Creek I saw that the tide was in; the swelling river was tossing little foaming waves upon the bit of beach and slapped idly at the wall of the jetty as if too sleepy to do more on this lovely afternoon. The water looked delicious: if I could get down to it I would sit in the pear-shaped boat that was still there, tied to the jetty, and imagine I was in a gondola in Venice — I'd never travelled abroad and Venice was my Mecca; the place I most wanted to visit.

The hillside was steeper than I'd thought; loose earth and stones rolled in front of me as I scrambled down, I was nearly rolling myself. I must have made some noise for the door of the checking office was opened and there was Edward. He ran towards me and as

I came slipping down the last slope of hillside he served as a barrier to stop me from running into the water, unable to stop. His strong arms steadied me and I apologised for my abrupt arrival; we were man and wife but we greeted each other like mere acquaintances, though pleased to meet. 'I haven't seen you down this way before,' he said. 'Of course the mill is too noisy week-days but it's nice here when we aren't working, and you like walking.'

There was really no reason why this was only the second time I'd come to the mill and the creek, but being embarrassed and nervous I said, foolishly, 'I thought I would be trespassing.'

'You cannot be a trespasser!' exclaimed Edward. 'You must remember that you belong here now, are part owner of all this, including the saw-mill. I said, 'With all my worldly goods I thee endow', and I meant it.'

I felt my cheeks blushing and was impatient with myself. Why was I being so silly just because Edward and I were alone together unexpectedly and away from the house? 'And I said 'obey'', I reminded him, though it had no point in the conversation.

'Yes, I require immediate obedience from you,' he laughed, teasing me and making me feel easier. 'Let's go down the river to the Point,' he suggested. 'We can call on Nanny Bullen; I promised her I'd take you there some time.'

I'd heard of Nanny Bullen from Aunt Ada. Nanny had been nursemaid to Edward's father and herself and Uncle Lando, and to their father before that; she was already too old for work when Edward was a boy but had regarded him as her charge too, and had been like a second grandmother to him. I'd thought she was dead, Aunt Ada spoke as if she was, but Edward told me now that she lived at Pen Point, farther down Hawken Creek, where a couple of cottages — once fishermen's homes — were now occupied by Nanny and a kindly neighbour who kept an eye on her.

He meant we should go down the creek in the peculiar boat and I wasn't sure I wanted to do that: I'd imagined sitting in it, dreaming, in shallow water and securely moored to the jetty but to ride into deep water might be dangerous. I suppose my face showed my feelings for he laughed, and said, 'Don't worry, it's perfectly safe,' as he pulled the boat to the beach and handed me in. 'I built this boat myself, years ago,' he told me, 'and although the shape is unorthodox it is quite seaworthy — or at least riverworthy.'

I sat nervously straight-backed on the plank seat while he sat opposite me and took up the oars. He had taken off his jacket for the rowing: he was my husband but I couldn't remember seeing him without a jacket, not even in hot weather, he always wore one in the house. The sleeves of his shirt were rolled to the elbows and the open neck, unbuttoned almost to the waist, revealed a bronzed, hairy chest; his muscles rippled with the pull of the oars. I told myself — For goodness' sake stop staring at him! Look at the scenery; admire the view farther afield, not this virile, non-husband! I averted my gaze and studied the banks of the river the Treworgey side where trees, oak and ash and a few pine, grew thickly together and right down to the water. 'Will those trees be cut for timber?' I asked, more for something to say than really wanting to know, for now that I'd stopped staring at Edward I knew he was staring at me.

'No,' he replied, 'those are what I term the natural woods. The trees we are cutting now were planted for that purpose years ago. Luckily, before my father died he saw the necessity for it, for making Treworgey productive. The days of estates that eat up capital and give little in return are over; few people can afford that now and if one wants to keep a family home in proper order there has to be some way of balancing the budget.'

I trailed my fingers in the emerald

water and relaxed. Except for the swish of the oars and the occasional squawk of a disturbed water bird there was a peaceful silence; then Edward said: 'You're looking very elegant this afternoon, Catherine.'

I was embarrassed by this remark and so made an ungracious reply: 'I'm glad you're pleased,' I said. 'You paid for it — through my allowance, I mean.'

He was really surprised and quite cross. 'You know that's not true! You more than earn your allowance with all the book-keeping and other work you do — you paid for your outfit yourself! And even if I had paid for your new clothes what would be wrong in that? You are my wife and it pleases me to see you in pretty things; now don't let's squabble about it, there's nothing more sordid than a married couple quarrelling over money matters.'

I agreed with him, but then we weren't an ordinary married couple.

The river curved and we came into deep shadow which after the sunshine was deadly cold and I couldn't help giving a shiver. Edward pulled the boat into the bank and insisted that I had his jacket over my shoulders and then briskly rowed us on till we came into sunshine again, and to a small jetty like the one at the saw-mill though this one was overgrown with elder and bramble bushes and wild flowers. He tied the boat to a rusty iron bar and helped me out. We climbed the slimy green steps and Edward pushed a way for us along a weed-grown path, through fluffy-seeding rose-bay and purple thistles. 'Mind you don't get scratched,' he warned me. 'Keep the coat on; mind your legs.' He looked down at my sunburned lower limbs and I found myself hoping he didn't think them too unshapely.

We came to a small grey cottage with blue woodsmoke twirling from the chimney and a garden full of faded summer flowers — roses that hadn't been pruned, lavender, honeysuckle and giant sunflowers. 'Nanny used to grow these for the birds and even though she can't do any gardening now they still come up after each year's seeding,' Edward told me, bending one of the drooping sunflowers so that I could see the thick head of purple-white seeds. He knocked on the cottage door then opened it without waiting for an answer and called, 'Anybody home? It's Edward come to see you, Nanny, and I've brought my wife.'

The front door led straight into a room where a little old lady sat before the fire in an old-fashioned basket-chair. Her hair was almost gone; her eyes were sunk far back in their sockets and clogged with crusted weepings from their weakness; the skin of her forehead and cheeks was deep rutted in long-life channels, very different from the soft pink powdered skin of Granny Constantine — though even more long-lasting than hers! Nanny wore a black dress and white apron, her hands lay on her lap in meek acceptance of their loss of usefulness, and she was so still that at first I thought she had died, there in her chair; then her eyes focused on us as we stood in the light from the window and a quavering voice said, 'Fancy you comin' at this time of day.'

'We came by boat, down the river,' said Edward.

'Fancy that!' said Nanny, weakly amazed.

'This is my wife, Catherine,' he told her, introducing me, and she tried to turn to see me better. I moved closer and took one of her frail hands in mine and gave it a squeeze. I didn't know if she could see me or not, her eyes looked sightless. 'Fancy that,' she quavered again.

'Does she mind living all alone?' I whispered to Edward, and surprisingly Nanny heard me too. 'Mrs. Smith sees to me,' she told me. 'She'll come to put me to bed soon.' She was stronger, mentally and physically, for a moment and twisted in her chair, trying to see the time by the grandfather clock in the corner of the room. She grumbled: 'All the times I've put others to bed — Miss Ada and Master Orlando, and their father before them — and now I've got to be put to bed myself! Fancy that!'

There was a tap at the door and a rosy-cheeked, bustling woman came in; surprised to see us but not put out about it. 'I've come to make her Bengers and put her to bed,' she told us. 'There's no sense in her being up after dark and the day will soon clap down on us once the sun's gone.' She poked the fire and the waiting kettle started to sing. Then she took a cup and saucer from the dresser and arranged them on a tray with a plate of biscuits and a slice of cheese in preparation for Nanny's supper. We felt in the way, the room was so small, and Edward said: 'We'll be going now, Nanny,' but Nanny's interest in us had faded in favour of those comforting companions, Bengers and bed; she hardly noticed our departure.

As Edward rowed us back up the river; having to strain harder this time against the pull of the receding tide, I thought about old age and wondered if I wanted to live to be as old as Nanny Bullen: the deteriorating body, rheumaticky limbs; the lessening of awareness, of intelligence; were not attractive to look forward to; yet all life is precious, more to the old than to the young who see years of it stretching endlessly, plentifully, fruitfully ahead: if Nanny heard the autumn song of the robin sometimes, or sniffed the scent of a rose — or even her pappy Bengers — with pleasure, then life was still sweet to her. 'How old is she?' I asked Edward.

'I'm not certain,' he replied. 'She must be very old indeed. Aunt Ada is the one to ask; she will tell you. She knows the family history better than I do, including the history of the servants, and remembers when there were more servants than family in residence at Treworgey. She knows all about the pets too: the pony that threw Uncle Lando was shot by my grandfather that same morning though who can say if the pony or the rider was at fault? Aunt Ada says Uncle Lando was a very daring boy and he might have been trying a jump that was too high. And she remembers the dogs they had and a parrot named Mr. Pecksniff that could ask, 'Got a cold?' Her interest in the past is confined to personal family things though, she had no patience with Granny's anecdotes which were more of the place than the people.'

I remembered how Granny had talked of the men and women buried in the churchyard and thought Edward a little wrong here, but the mention of dogs had made me think of Jasper; he hadn't been with us that afternoon. 'Where's Jasper today?' I asked, and he replied, 'He's asleep in the checking shed. He likes it there, it smells of cats, and although he's too slow to catch them now he likes to lie there and dream of past, exciting chases.'

Edward's Land-Rover was at the mill — he used this on work days and when on the woodland tracks, it was more suitable than the Bentley — and he took me the road way home, a new way for me; not the proper road that led to Treluz Major but a rough-surface road that led straight to the house. He stopped for me to get out before driving round to the garage and as he opened the door for me I handed him back his jacket and said, 'I've missed tea and if we're not careful we'll be late for dinner' — we had our evening meal early on Sundays. 'Aunt Ada will wonder where we've been together this time of day.'

He grinned and slammed the car door shut. 'Fancy that!' he said, gently mocking Nanny Bullen, and as he drove away I hurried up the steps and into the house feeling, for the first time, I think, that I really belonged there; and that Edward and I had broken — or at least bent a little — the barrier between us; the absurd barrier of too-careful courtesy on his part and awkward shyness on mine.

6

I grew very fond of Aunt Ada, and of Mimsy too, and I think they were fond of me; I hadn't tried to alter their way of life in any way and my praise and appreciation was welcome to them, they'd borne the brunt of the domestic side of Treworgey for years, with little thanks it seemed to me.

I felt as if Aunt Ada were my mother — I hardly remembered my real mother, I was so young when she died — and one day when we were having our after-lunch cup of tea she said to me: 'You're like a daughter to me, Catherine. I know I've said it before, but I wish I'd had a daughter, they're so much more satisfactory than sons.'

'Doesn't your son, Trevor, come home sometimes?' I asked.

'No. Edward banished him from Treworgey; but he was justified in doing so.'

Was any reason good enough to separate a mother from her son? I found myself criticizing Edward; sometimes he was too severe.

'You see,' continued Aunt Ada, 'Trevor was a late-born baby, he came when we'd resigned ourselves to being childless, and we spoilt him. Then when his father died I spoilt him more than ever. He was clever but he wouldn't put his mind to his studies; was lazy and didn't seem to care what he did; didn't want to go to college or university. So eventually Edward got him a job in the bank, the Treluz Major bank that he dealt with himself. We thought all was going well, then it was discovered that about three hundred pounds had been misappropriated by Trevor: he owned up when they had the investigation. It was a difficult situation for Edward, it being his banking place and his cousin that he'd recommended. He paid the missing money from his own account and the affair was kept out of the court but he insisted that Trevor leave

Treworgey and I think Trevor was glad to go.'

'Does he write to you?'

'Only an occasional post-card, those sick-joke kind. He doesn't remember me at Christmas or on my birthday. He has a little money of his own from his father's will, enough to keep him from starving if he's not in work, but he'd developed rather expensive tastes, one way and another, so I'm always afraid he'll get into more trouble.'

I tried to comfort her: I told her that young people were restless nowadays, and adventurous, and didn't stay at home like they used to do. She wept a few tears, my sympathy having made her feel sorry for herself I think, then blew her nose noisily and smiled at me. 'Never mind,' she said, 'I've got *you* now,' and I smiled back and poured her another cup of tea.

It was only a week or two after this conversation that my troubles began; the period of serenity was over. One sunny morning I decided to go to see

Nanny Bullen: I knew the way through the woods to her cottage now and visited her quite often because by keeping an eye on her I was helping Edward who considered himself responsible for all Treworgey's employees, past and present; knowing I'd been there he didn't have to do any checking-up himself. As I walked along I picked Nanny a few sprays of spindle, hoping that even her poor old eyes would be able to see the bursting pink and orange brightness of the berries. When I put them into her claw-like hands she smiled with pleasure and tried to raise them to her nose to smell. She probably didn't know what it was I'd given her so I said, 'It's spindle berry, Nanny.' 'Fancy that,' she replied.

I sat opposite her and we had our usual mostly one-sided conversation, with me shouting her snippets of news from Treworgey, making much of little sometimes to entertain her, and she nodding her agreement or approval. Then I went out to the tiny back scullery to look for a vase or jam-jar to use to put the spindle in water. There was a shelf with black iron pots and pans, a tap and old brown stoneware sink, and a wash-boiler of the kind that has to have a fire lit under it; there was a wooden cover to the boiler, it served as a draining-board, and on it were two unwashed cups and saucers and a partly-used packet of biscuits. Who had been drinking cups of tea with Nanny? As far as I knew no one but Edward and myself and Mrs. Smith, the neighbour, came to the cottage and Mrs. Smith was always too busy to stop for cups of tea; and if she had done so would never have left the china unwashed, I knew she made sure all was clean and tidy at the cottage before leaving. I was alarmed. I looked towards the stairs, winding wooden stairs that led from the small space between the two rooms: I'd never been up them but supposed there was another bedroom besides the one Nanny slept in; was someone up there now, hiding, waiting for me to go?

I found a jar and arranged the spindle twigs and took them to Nanny. I wanted to question her about the teacups but didn't feel I had the right to, especially if the reason for them was an innocent, easily-explained one; and would I be able to make her understand? I tried to chat to her about other things but couldn't stay there imagining that someone was listening. Nanny didn't seem upset or frightened; I was being silly; but would tell Edward and see what he said.

I wished Nanny good-bye and hurried back through the woods. I'd not gone far, though, when I heard someone running after me and, suppressing the desire to break into a run myself, I stopped and waited. My pursuer was a young man, a pretty young man with long blond girlish curls held in place with a headband or braid — it was purple and white with golden stars spaced round and reminded me of the gay-coloured circlets used on Christmas cakes. He wore a purple shirt and tight trousers under a shapeless and dirty sheepskin coat with the woolly side uppermost — perhaps it wasn't sheepskin for the wool wasn't curly but long and hairy. But he wasn't a wolf for when he caught up with me he was polite and spoke with a soft, well-educated voice. 'You are Mrs. Constantine, aren't you; the new Mrs. Constantine?' he asked. 'Let me introduce myself: I'm Trevor Drummond, my mother is at Treworgey. Perhaps she's spoken of me.'

'Yes, I'm Mrs. Constantine,' I replied. 'And your mother has told me about you.' I remembered the regretful way in which Aunt Ada had referred to her son and I added, 'She would like to see you. Are you coming back to the house with me now?'

'No, I can't do that, Cousin Edward wouldn't allow it' — he said this offhandedly as if his banishment didn't matter to him, and continued, 'Don't tell Mother I'm here, it would only upset her. But there *is* something I'd like you to do for me — give this note to Victor, I believe he's still with Uncle Lando. Do it so that nobody else knows, and don't tell anyone you've seen me, please!'

I suppose I should have refused to be involved in such secrecy, should have told Trevor to get his note delivered by some other means; to post it; certainly I didn't agree to be messenger for Trevor's sake; but deep down I considered Edward's refusal to have him at Treworgey was too harsh, particularly for Aunt Ada, and by delivering the note I would be making my gesture of protest. I took the envelope and put it in my pocket.

'Thanks a lot!' said Trevor, and he turned back towards the cottage. I called after him: 'You're not being a nuisance to Nanny Bullen, are you?'

'Don't worry about that,' he answered. 'She loves me — she loves all the family. She lived her life for them and would die for them, poor bloody sod!' He was less of a gentleman with his 'poor bloody sod' but he didn't sound unkind: I needn't worry about Nanny's welfare. And there was still Mrs. Smith to look after her — she must think we knew Trevor was at the cottage. No, I needn't worry about Nanny, but began to worry about the note in my pocket and hurried home to get rid of it as soon as possible.

I waited for Victor on the landing. I knew him better now but still didn't like him much; I hadn't realised that he would know Trevor but he'd been with Uncle Lando for some years and must have been at Treworgey when Trevor was still at home. Aunt Ada rang the gong with her usual noisy enthusiasm and soon he and Uncle Lando came down the stairs. I passed him the note. 'It's from Trevor,' I whispered, and he looked at me in surprise, surprise that I should be a party to intrigue I expect, and put it in his pocket unopened.

I took my place at table feeling guilty though it wasn't anything very terrible I'd done. My face was inclined to reveal my emotions and when Edward enquired casually, 'What have you been up to this morning, Catherine?' the way he put the question made me imagine he knew something was wrong. I told him: 'I was up-to-date with the book-keeping so walked over to Pen Point to see Nanny.'

'How was she?' he asked.

I hadn't changed my place at table, I still sat opposite Uncle Lando and Victor, and I could sense that Victor was especially interested in my answer, was waiting to see if I would mention Trevor. This was the moment to forget my promise to Trevor — if I *had* promised — and to announce that he was at the Point, but all I said was, 'Oh, she seemed all right, Edward; the same as usual.'

'Good,' he said, and turned to take his plate from Aunt Ada. He had no reason to suppose my visit to Nanny was different to other times; and perhaps, also, I was attaching too much importance to Trevor's presence at the cottage.

But I was less happy now; I couldn't forget my small deceit and thinking about it destroyed my peace of mind. I felt I'd let Edward down and avoided him whenever possible; yet if I'd run to him tale-telling against Trevor surely I would have been feeling guilty towards Aunt Ada?

No, I was right and Edward was wrong! He was too harsh in his judgements; unkind to his aunt and her son; it was preposterous to keep them apart! Trevor hadn't wanted to see his mother and I thought that was bad, and he ought not to be on the Treworgey estate in secret, but I tried to convince myself that Edward was the real 'villain of the piece'.

7

Several times during the next week I wondered if I ought to tell Aunt Ada I'd met her son so that she could try to see him herself, but I was afraid this might be doing more harm than good for Trevor hadn't wanted to see his mother; besides, he might have left the district by now, there was no sign of him at Nanny Bullen's cottage when I checked a few days later: I decided not to tell her — and I persuaded myself it was too late to tell Edward. Victor continued in his usual silent, enigmatic way and sometimes it seemed as if I'd dreamt the encounter with Trevor.

Then one night, a Friday night, we were wakened by a loud knocking on the door. Treworgey had no bell to be rung but the big brass lion-head knocker was being hammered continually, with a thumping accompaniment of fist on wood as someone tried to rouse us. As I lay in bed, struggling out of dreams and identifying the noise, Edward dashed through the room in his pyjamas and dressing-gown. I got out of bed and slipping on my gown hurried downstairs too.

Edward had admitted Tom Pacey who was in a very agitated state. 'It's fire at the mill!' he was exclaiming. 'The wind's more our way, to the village, than here and we were woke up by the smell, and we could see the blaze from our bedroom window! And the car's not in the garage! It was gone when I got the Land-Rover out and' — but Edward was already phoning to Treluz Major for the fire brigade.

Aunt Ada and Mimsy who had heard the commotion too, but had taken longer to make themselves respectable, joined us in the hall and, not knowing what to do to help, pestered Tom for more information which he was unable to give. He and Edward hurried from the house and I followed them. They were climbing into the Land-Rover and I shouted, 'Wait for me, I'm coming too!'

But Edward shouted in reply: 'Go back to bed at once, Catherine! You'll catch cold out here!' And he drove off down the road to the mill.

How could I go back to bed! And although November it wasn't a cold night: I ran after them. The road was rough but very straight; built up, with ditches at each side and lined with trees; a full moon made the way clear. I could smell the fire now but the main smoke was blowing more to the west, to Hawken village, as Tom had said. Twice I scrambled down into the ditch as first the fire-engine and then an ambulance raced bumpily along the road; they had come via Hawken and the house, the drivers perhaps being uncertain of the saw-mill location. I was wearing dark blue pyjamas and dressing-gown and wasn't observed; I hid because there was no sense in causing them to stop to discover who I was or for information concerning the fire; I didn't want to be a hindrance.

It was farther to the mill than I'd thought and before I got there the ambulance passed me again, branching to the 'new' road this time, on its way back; but I didn't worry, thinking possibly it was sent out automatically to any fire and, finding no one in danger, was returning to Treluz Major; the small town would only have one ambulance and other calls might come in. But when at last I reached the yard I found Tom Pacey very upset. He said: 'Mr. Edward thought Jasper was in the checking shed — he'd left him there when he locked up — and he must needs go in to rescue him! The dog wasn't there, had probably run out of his own accord long before, and Mr. Edward only got out again just in time then the roof fell in; as it is he's got bad burns on his hands and feet, and a crack on the head as well, somehow. They've taken him to hospital.'

If anyone could have known my

reaction to this news they would have judged me to be a real wife to Edward for my heart thumped alarmingly; I felt faint at his lack of caution — bravery, I suppose it was — in entering the burning shed; I was worried, very worried, about his injuries: shock, I'd been told, was often the cause of death rather than the burns in a case like this — he might die! He was a kind husband, I liked and respected him and in some ways admired him in spite of the times he was domineering or unreasonable — he mustn't die!

Tom put an arm round me as we stood there watching the blaze which the firemen had under control now, it was not going to reach the main timber piles and at this time of year there was little danger to the woods, the growing trees, for the damp night air extinguished the flying sparks before they could do damage. 'Don't worry,' Tom comforted me. 'Mr. Edward will be all right, he's tough. You go on back to the house. I must stay to see the end of this; he told me to.'

So I started on my way home, running as much as I could then slowing till my breath came back. Half way to Treworgey Jasper ran out of the woods to join me. I stopped a moment to welcome him and found that his collar was loose — but it wasn't his collar that hung floppingly round his neck: it was the purple-and-white, starry headband I'd last seen keeping Trevor's curls in place! I knew then that the fire had not been accidental: it was the work of Trevor, thinking to 'get his own back' on Edward, or perhaps just one of the meaningless, destructive actions he and young people of his kind could think a huge joke.

I slipped the headband into my dressing-gown pocket and hurried on with poor old Jasper panting behind me, determined to keep up. When we reached the house the ambulance was outside and I found Aunt Ada in the hall talking to the ambulance men who seemed glad to see me. 'Are you Mrs.

Constantine?' asked one of them, and when I replied 'Yes', he said, 'Then let me tell *you* what's happened.' He implied that Aunt Ada was in too agitated a state to absorb information.

'Your husband has bad burns on his hands and feet,' I was told. 'We took him to hospital for treatment but he refused to stay there so we brought him home again. He's had a sedative and is sleeping now but you must be careful with him, burns can be nasty. The dressings must be changed, his doctor or the district nurse will see to that, and there's more pills for him, but you must see that he takes them and that he stays in bed and keeps still to give the burns a chance to heal — by tonight's behaviour I can see he's a very stubborn man!' My informant smiled at me and I was reassured: Edward wasn't too bad, they wouldn't have brought him home if his life was in danger.

Mimsy had made hot coffee and sandwiches for the ambulance men and they sat down with her for a minute or two of relaxation from duty. I went upstairs to Edward, closely followed by Aunt Ada. When I opened the bedroom door my husband was lying on his back, white-faced except for a reddish-blue bruise on his forehead; his bandage-swathed hands were stretched out over the top of the eiderdown and there was a hump at the end of the bed where some sort of cage arrangement — later I found this to be a fire-guard — kept the weight of the bedclothes from his feet. And he was in *my* bed, the big double bed we were supposed to be sleeping in together but which was *my* bed! Now that I knew Edward was all right, had no very terrible injuries, I think the fact that he was in that bed was a greater shock than the rest of the night's happenings put together! But Aunt Ada didn't know this — mustn't know this. To her he was in his right place and she'd probably shown the men where to put him. 'I'll sleep in the dressing-room,' I told her, 'but let's go down and have some coffee with the others, there's nothing we can do for Edward at the moment, is there?'

'No, I suppose not,' she agreed tearfully as we descended the stairs. 'Why did this have to happen! Everything was going so well for him now, married to you. He was happier than I've ever known him; he was solemn and over-conscientious even as a boy, and then he had the family cares and responsibilities thrust on him too young; he's never had time to be happy.'

'Never mind, it's not too bad,' I comforted her. 'You know how strong he is, he will soon get over this.' I couldn't tell her that I believed her irresponsible, neglectful son to be the cause of Edward's present condition.

I took Jasper to the library for the night; he, too, needed to sleep off his night's adventure. Then, after coffee and consolations with Aunt Ada and Mimsy I returned upstairs and, carefully tiptoeing past the sleeping Edward, got into the narrow dressing-room bed recently occupied by him. I imagined the sheets were still warm from his body and as, over-tired and upset, I slipped into sleep myself I half believed he was there beside me.

8

I wondered afterwards why, that night, none of us had thought of Victor. He was a kind of nurse, a male nurse, and would have been a help to the ambulance men when they had to get Edward to bed; and his presence would have calmed Aunt Ada who, frightened and tearful, had been useless in the emergency. In the morning we learnt that he wouldn't have been available to help: he had packed his belongings and was gone from Treworgey! He must have left after dinner, after getting Uncle Lando to bed, and perhaps it was he who had appropriated the Bentley which was found abandoned on the Plymouth road five or six miles beyond Treluz Major; the police had reported this by telephone and were coming to make enquiries, and to look into the cause of the fire. They might not see any connection between the theft of the car and the fire, but I did: I believed that Trevor and Victor had been companions in making trouble for us and had used the car to get away.

After our breakfast Mimsy brought in a tray with breakfast for Edward. I wished Aunt Ada would take it up to him but it was obvious that they expected me to do so. When I entered the bedroom Edward was awake and sitting up in bed — when I passed through earlier he'd still been sleeping — and Tom Pacey was there and had just washed and shaved him. Tom must also have told him of Victor's disappearance and was promising to look after Uncle Lando, saying, 'Don't you fret, about him, sir, I'll go straight to tend him now,' and smiling and wishing me 'Good-morning, ma'am,' he left the room.

In the dressing-room bed the night before I'd slept easily at first but had wakened early and, unable to sleep again, had relived the night's happenings and knew I must now tell Edward about my meeting with Trevor and taking Victor the note; the finding of Trevor's headband round Jasper's neck; and my beliefs regarding the cause of the fire. Now that Victor had decamped I was certain he'd been in league with Trevor, that they'd plotted together and set fire to the checking shed. I wasn't sure if they'd intended Jasper to perish: they might have and he'd escaped. There'd been the theft from the bank too: possibly Victor had a hand in that, encouraging Trevor to 'cook the books' and helping him to use the money. Because I didn't like Victor it was easy to make him a villain, but I was sure I was right.

So, as with some embarrassment I fed Edward the thinly-cut bread and butter and soft-boiled eggs prepared by Mimsy, I told him about the dirty cups and saucers at Nanny Bullen's and about meeting Trevor and taking back the secret note to Victor.

I expected Edward to be cross with me but was glad his anger gathered slowly, I didn't want his temperature to rise. He said, consideringly, 'That explains Victor's surliness; and perhaps he'd been meeting Trevor in Plymouth, he went there so often lately.' Then his tone changed and he exclaimed, 'Why didn't you tell me you'd seen Trevor, Catherine! I should have been prepared for trouble if I'd known he was about. Why didn't you tell me, you silly girl!'

'I thought you were cruel to keep Aunt Ada and Trevor apart; he's her son!'

'Don't talk about things you don't understand! Aunt Ada is happy enough as she is, Trevor only worries and disappoints her. Mother-and-son love isn't automatic, you know. She feels sentimental at times and persuades herself that all was well between them but in fact as soon as he was in long trousers he defied her and was a pain in the neck to all of us. I'm considerably older than Trevor but she and I are more a mother and son than they ever were.' He paused and I gave him another sip of tea, then he asked: 'Have you told anyone else about your meeting with Trevor?'

'No,' I replied.

'Then don't mention it to a soul, least of all to Aunt Ada: what she doesn't know she can't worry over. Don't talk about Victor's disappearance more than you can help either. I don't want anyone to perjure themselves but the less said about that the better. Tom Pacey will be discreet, and Aunt Ada, if the police question her, will make such a muddle of her replies that little notice will be taken of what she says. I doubt if they — the police — will find any proof of arson, and they may treat the theft of the car as a separate matter. They don't know about Trevor being here and they needn't learn about Victor, or at least not that he departed without our knowledge. For Aunt Ada's sake the matter will be best left unsolved — apparently there's no damage to the car, it was merely out of petrol and left at the roadside. I expect Victor *did* take it but he's unlikely to bother us again and, but for the way he departed, I can't say I'm sorry to see the back of him. He did his job well enough but there was something about him I couldn't fathom, though I didn't know there'd been any particular friendship with Trevor.'

I thought of Uncle Lando, now without his 'keeper', and I said, eager to make amends for my silence regarding Trevor, 'I'll look after Uncle Lando. We get on well together.'

Edward looked at me with what I thought was staring sternness and I was unable to remove my gaze from his; I was mesmerised. He said: 'You, my girl, will look after me! Aunt Ada will expect it of you, a loving wife, and I require it too. Take it to be a punishment if you like. And as for Uncle Lando — you only see him at his best; there are things a man must do for him.' He twisted his face away as I tried to make him swallow more tea. 'This is what I want you to do,' he continued: 'Phone

Latimer Lodge the home for people mentally ill, and see if they've a man available for an outside job — Victor came to us from there and really I've no quarrel with his treatment of Uncle Lando — they will probably send someone, they know what's required and we pay well. You are to give whoever comes an interview to see what you think and engage him if he's suitable: I'll rely on your judgement. And we want someone as soon as possible of course; Tom Pacey has enough on his hands, one way and another!'

'Yes, Edward,' I replied obediently, trying to sound humble, penitent; and Edward gave me a look as if to say, 'I hope you mean it!' I plumped up his pillows and smoothed the eiderdown, bending over him. He shut his eyes as if not wishing to see me, then said crossly, 'Leave it; that's good enough! Now go and do that phoning. And when the police come send them up to me; try to keep them away from Aunt Ada — and stop her from sick-visiting me if that's possible, her sympathy will make me irritable.' I thought: You're irritable enough already!

I took the breakfast tray and left the room: the cares of Treworgey were on my shoulders now. That morning must have been the busiest, most worrying morning I'd ever had! First I told Aunt Ada, who was 'just going to pop up to see Edward', that he was having a nap and shouldn't be disturbed; then I phoned Latimer Lodge and, luckily, they had an attendant free — a Mr. Best — and he would come over to see us next morning; then the doctor came and spent a long time upstairs with Edward, but as he left he told me that the burns were clean, there was no danger of infection, and as my husband was in good health they would heal rapidly as long as he was patient and didn't try to hurry things by getting up too soon; I must keep him in bed. Almost as soon as I'd shown him to the door the police arrived. They were two young, fresh-faced constables and I felt I could deal with them: I told them what I knew of the fire, and of the damage done, but they thought the damage was more a matter for the insurance people than themselves; then I said that the Treluz Major garage mechanic had reported the car to be in good order and was bringing it back to us that afternoon; I didn't speak of Victor's disappearance and neither did the policemen — they even may not have been aware of his existence. Fortunately Aunt Ada didn't mention him either, but let me do the talking.

Then I took the constables up to Edward and what transpired there I don't know. As they left they said, enigmatically, that there were a few more enquiries to make: I took this to mean Tom Pacey was to be questioned for they drove off towards the mill and I knew he was down there checking on the extent of the damage and seeing if it was possible for the men to start work as usual on Monday — he didn't work at the mill, of course, but was familiar with what went on there and could bring back a report to Edward. Before lunch I took Jasper for a walk round the garden; although he came rather unwillingly it was a breathing space for me, a chance to lose some of my nervous tension. We met Tom on his way back from the mill and I asked him if the mill cats were all right and he told me they were. He said: 'Yes, ma'am, I've counted them. They're a bit extra shy but they're all there. I took down some milk and coaxed them out of hiding.' I was relieved; I wouldn't have liked that happy colony to be harmed.

I took Edward's lunch up to the bedroom and as I fed him I had a funny feeling he was enjoying the situation, as if by making me wait on him he was subduing me, disciplining me, though as far as I knew I'd never aggravated him or gone against his wishes: I'd kept quiet about meeting Trevor and taking Victor the note, but that was all. I spent the afternoon with Uncle Lando and, perhaps because he sensed something was wrong and that Victor's absence was more than just a day off, he wasn't on his usual-with-me good behaviour. I had a trying time with him; he refused to be interested in his jigsaw puzzles or ludo, and towards the end of the afternoon crawled under the table and made squeaking noises at me: I couldn't tell whether his fat body was wedged there or if he was only playing. I realised that Edward was right, I couldn't have looked after Uncle Lando fulltime, he needed someone to be firm, even stern, with him, and after the easy-going pattern of our other times together I was unable to establish authority and was thankful when Tom Pacey came to take over.

At dinner-time as I ladled him spoonfuls of soup Edward said, 'You look tired, Catherine. Go to bed early, my dear.' Then he remembered that he occupied what had been my bed and added: 'Can you sleep in that other bed? It's smaller; is it comfortable enough?'

I was cross with him. He knew that the dressing-room bed was quite comfortable; he was so much bigger than me and if he could sleep in it why shouldn't I? 'Of course it's all right,' I said testily, and slammed the door as I left the room. Later, creeping past him on my way to bed, was he sleeping peacefully with a smile on his face and laughing at me in this dreams?

The next morning I interviewed Mr. Best from Latimer Lodge and, having been coached by Edward, managed very well I thought. Mr. Best was about thirty years old, fair-haired and pink-cheeked, very different from the dark, bearded Victor; and he was so garrulous I felt I knew his life story after our first quarter of an hour together. I decided he would suit us for surely no man as guileless as he appeared to be would plot a fire in the wood yard or the theft of our car. He'd brought a small suitcase and was prepared to stay, saying he could send for the rest of his things, so I took him up to his room and then in to the old nursery to meet Uncle Lando. These two fell in love with each other straight away.

As the weeks passed and he inserted himself into our lives, I wasn't really sure I liked Mr. Best — Ronnie; but he charmed Aunt Ada and Mimsy with his ever-ready platitudes, and I was satisfied with his care of Uncle Lando though he treated his charge rather as a great big doll, to be washed and dressed and played with, and didn't try to develop the retarded mind — but perhaps this didn't matter, I'd learnt there was a stage of understanding beyond which Uncle Lando couldn't advance. And I tried to forgive Ronnie his effusiveness, his desire to know everything and let everything be known, for I understood from my own earlier years what it was like to be lonely and want to be part of a family.

I think Edward judged Ronnie as I did: I introduced Ronnie to his new employer that first morning and left them to get acquainted and when I took

Edward his lunch, later, he said: 'He'll do; he's the *best* we can expect, I suppose,' emphasising 'best' as Ronnie's surname and making a joke for me to smile at.

He — Edward — was taking his enforced idleness very well. I'd expected him to resent inactivity, to fret and fume that he couldn't be in on-the-spot control of things; of course he had the mill foreman come to consult him and he gave his instructions, and when the farm manager phoned to ask how Edward was getting on I relayed a few messages regarding farm matters, but apart from this he relaxed and behaved almost as if on holiday. Tom Pacey came three or four times a day to attend to his personal needs but otherwise I was 'nurse'. As soon as he was able he edged himself out of bed after lunch and spent the afternoons in an easy chair with his feet on a stool — the doctor had said I must keep him in bed, but how could I? I couldn't tie him down. We played Scrabble, with me arranging both lots of letters on the board and not taking advantage of my knowledge of the letters he had; it wasn't a very satisfactory way of playing but it amused him as he always managed to win. Aunt Ada had a habit of popping in for a chat and once Ronnie brought Uncle Lando, shining-faced and eager to please, to visit us, so to avoid these interruptions Edward told me to lock the bedroom door. I did this reluctantly: 'What will they think of us?' I asked, not really requiring a reply. But Edward laughed and told me, 'They'll think I'm making love to you, as much as I can manage with these handicaps, and so will leave us alone.' I knew my colour was rising and couldn't look at him; I purposely dropped the box of Scrabble letters I was carrying to the table and recovering these gave me a chance to recover my composure too.

I felt Edward was teasing me these days — and nights! However late I stayed up he would be awake when I went to bed. He would stare me through the room and then, as I clicked off the light he would call, 'Goodnight, Catherine'. Sometimes he would pretend to be asleep and I would tiptoe carefully and then he would open his eyes and, laughing at me, say, 'You're late!' or 'I thought you were never coming; good-night', and I wanted to slam the dressing-room door in protest — and would have done so far as he was concerned but I didn't want to disturb the other occupants of Treworgey; or give them cause to wonder why I did so. Sometimes I wondered what was the matter with Edward and me: we were behaving like children!

9

In the middle of December Edward moved back to the dressing-room and I returned to the double bed; he'd been up and about for several days, the forehead bruise was fading, the bandages had been removed from his hands and feet, and he was restless. One morning after breakfast he appeared dressed for out of doors: it was a bitterly cold morning and Aunt Ada and I were alarmed that he was going out. He was going to the mill to see how the repair of the checking shed was progressing, he told us, and we tried to persuade him not to go: 'You're not strong enough yet,' we said.

This made him cross. 'Of course I'm strong enough!' he argued. 'I didn't have a heart attack and there's nothing wrong with my lungs! I was burnt and now my wounds are healed.'

I looked at his hands: new soft pink flesh instead of the hard calloused palms! I winced at the thought of the use he might make of them, hauling timber. 'You had a bump on the head too,' I said, still trying to dissuade him.

'And did that make me silly in the head?' he asked, his grey eyes searching mine, and I thought there was some double meaning to his words: was he reminding me of his teasing behaviour these last few weeks? I didn't answer, and Aunt Ada said, 'Of course you're not silly in the head — that's poor Lando — but we *shall* think you silly if you go down there and do too much and make yourself ill again. Catherine has checked and everything is going well, you don't have to worry about it.'

Edward looked at me questioningly and I said: 'I've been there a couple of times: once when the insurance people were here and once to see if one of the orders — for fencing posts — had been dispatched before the fire; there was an enquiry concerning them.'

'I thought I said you were not to go down there when the men are about!' he stormed, ignoring the help I'd given. 'You disobeyed me!'

'So I did!' I replied quite cheekily, for he was making a fuss about nothing. 'The men were very nice to me; one of them gave me some tea from his thermos.'

'Do you mean to say you've been picnicking with the workmen!'

I giggled at the thought of that and might have tried to explain how I'd been at the yard during the morning tea-break and the men had come to ask me how he, 'the boss', was recovering from his accident, then they'd offered me their tea and biscuits and it would have been rude to refuse; but Aunt Ada had sprung to my defence: 'Dear Catherine has been splendid!' she declared. 'She's helped in every possible way, besides having to nurse you!'

'I know, I know! I don't deserve such a perfect wife.'

This was just the kind of remark that

Aunt Ada liked; it fitted her picture of us as a happily-married pair. I was certain he was being sarcastic and gave him what I hoped was a defiant glare but found he was looking at me quite sincerely as if he'd meant what he said. I was glad that Mimsy started to clear the table and I helped her while Aunt Ada followed Edward out of the house shouting precautions.

It was only two weeks to Christmas now and the Treworgey kitchen was a hive of activity; the larder and fridge and cupboards were packed with seasonal extras and Mimsy, mixing her second lot of puddings, filled the air with the delicious smell of raisins and rum. This holiday wasn't being regarded as 'the first Christmas without Granny' but as 'Catherine's first Christmas at Treworgey'. Strangely, I think Granny was remembered less because she had lived so long. As with other old people, even great artists or writers or states-men, she had slipped away almost unnoticed I sometimes felt. Such persons, if they'd died suddenly in middle age, would have annexed the front-page headlines and had their full achievements recorded; but twenty or thirty years on, having retired into oblivion and being thought by many to be already dead, they only received half a column on an inside page. Although I hadn't known Granny for long I'd been her close companion during our short friendship and I still thought of her a lot: perhaps I was wrong in thinking the others didn't remember her enough but none of them wanted to talk about her — except Tom Pacey, and he and I did sometimes have a chat about 'the old lady', as he called her.

But this was to be my 'first Christmas' and Aunt Ada and Mimsy were determined I should enjoy it, especially as Edward was nearly well again and things were back to normal according to Aunt Ada — I think she supposed that Edward and I were in double-bed contact again. She wanted us to give a party: 'It would be like old times, we always had a party,' she told me. She and Mimsy were so keen on the idea I didn't like to disappoint them but relied on Edward to dissuade them: unfortunately he thought a party would please me and gave them the O.K. on it. 'Who will come?' I asked Aunt Ada, and she replied, 'Oh the Vicar and the doctor, of course, and the folks from the big houses round here who've known Edward and the family for years. It's time we were sociable again and that you should meet people.'

I couldn't understand why we suddenly needed to be sociable. Except for in church on Sunday mornings we'd hardly seen or spoken to anyone but those associated with Treworgey; our wedding had been a very quiet affair, and all along I'd believed that, although Edward was civic-minded and had his say in local politics, the Constantines kept out of the limelight on account of Uncle Lando: a mentally deficient person, through whatever cause, presented problems, even sometimes meant ostracism.

But now we were to be sociable! I remembered Edward's remark when he proposed to me, never thought of again till now, that the 'gentry' round here — as well as Aunt Ada — had been trying to find a marriage partner for him. Were these the people who would be coming to the party? They would think me a poor substitute for one of their pretty, clever daughters! I dreaded the party and pushed the thought of it to the back of my mind to be dealt with later; the party was not to be held till after Christmas.

By the way Aunt Ada and Mimsy whispered together and hustled things out of sight when I entered the little sitting-room unexpectedly it was obvious they were giving me a present and I would have to give them something too. I wanted to give them presents, I was very fond of them, but what on earth could I give? All their needs were supplied by Treworgey, except clothes, but it would be unwise to buy either an article of apparel, they had peculiar tastes in jumpers and cardigans; and they probably had drawers full of hankies and scarves and gloves. Aunt Ada was fond of chocolates and crystallized fruits but had these sent from Fortnum and Mason so extras in that line would be no treat; neither of them did much reading so books wouldn't be particularly welcome, and to give Mimsy a cookery book, though there were such beautiful ones on sale now, would seem an insult to her splendid cooking: I decided that jewellery was the best thing to give them. I borrowed Tom Pacey and the Bentley and had a day's shopping in Treluz Major. I bought pretty sparkling brooches for Aunt Ada and Mimsy, a dashing psychedelic tie for Ronnie, a new kind of jigsaw for Uncle Lando — a three-dimensional one, a giant multicoloured cube to be taken apart and reassembled — and tobacco for Tom. I wondered if Edward would expect a gift from me: what could I give him? I could think of nothing better than a tie for him, too, though not a gaudy one like Ronnie's but a sober maroon with silver stripes. I didn't know if Edward would give me anything but if he did I was prepared, otherwise I could hide the tie and not embarrass him by presenting it.

When I went downstairs on Christmas morning I found there were packages beside our breakfast plates so I hastily fetched my presents and put them in their places, including Edward's tie for there was quite a large flat box addressed 'To Catherine' in his handwriting for me. As we drank our first cup of coffee we opened our gifts. I had the largest pile, for everyone had given me a present including Uncle Lando who was having Christmas-morning breakfast with us today; I was the only one to receive anything from him. Ronnie, determined to be a part of the family, had given something to all of us and I was thankful I'd bought him the tie, though Aunt Ada had remembered him too, and he also had Edward's cheque-containing envelope beside his plate — the others had envelopes too and I knew they contained cheques because I'd filled and addressed them for Edward.

I opened Uncle Lando's present first because he was obviously eager that I should. The writing on the package, poor man, was like that of a little child: large uneven letters saying, 'Merry Xmas from Uncle Lando', and even so this message had probably had the guidance of Ronnie's firmer hand, and there was a pathetic attempt at a painting of holly in red and green blobs to underline the inscription. Although Ronnie made no effort to improve the understanding of his charge he was a great one for occupational therapy and their room was filled with unrecognisable clay models, cut-outs from comics pasted on cardboard to make pictures, and collections of pebbles and scraps of pottery found in the garden: it really was remarkable what they had produced in the short time since Ronnie's arrival. He — Ronnie — had a stock of little sayings such as 'Idle hands make idle thoughts' and 'Be a busy bee and time flies'. I was often irritated by Uncle Lando's new 'keeper' but I think his attitude was the right one, his charge was happier than he'd been with Victor. Now, as I unwrapped the gift, I wasn't surprised that it was hand-made: it was a necklace of varnished rose hips threaded on a string with a bow of ribbon for fastening. I thanked Uncle Lando and hung it round my neck but apparently this was wrong for he stretched across the table and, taking the 'beads', clumsily wound them through my hair and round my head. Another kind of headband! For a fleeting moment I wondered if he'd ever seen the one Trevor had worn — now hidden amongst my hankies upstairs — and was alarmed at the thought of them meeting; then I remembered that Uncle Lando was Trevor's uncle too, of course they knew each other, they'd lived in the same house for many years — how silly of me to forget that. As I leaned over, allowing Uncle Lando to arrange his gift, I gave him a kiss on his flabby pink chin; he sat back in his chair so pleased and puffed up with pride I thought he might burst.

The others had been watching us but now began to attend to their own parcels. I continued opening mine and found a pink crocheted woollen jumper from Aunt Ada and an almost identical one in mauve from Mimsy. They may not have known it, but these kind of long shapeless jumpers were fashionable and I was delighted and profuse in my thanks; there was a lot of work — and a lot of hiding from view — involved in their production. Ronnie had given me a set of pencils and that left only Edward's gift to be unwrapped. I didn't know what to expect as I untied the cord and raised the cover of the box and unfolded the layers of tissue paper. It was something pink, flimsy and lacy: was it an evening dress? I lifted the garment from its packing and held it up. 'It's a nightie!' exclaimed Aunt Ada admiringly.

Well, it wasn't black nylon or see-through but although the skirt was long and full there was very little at the top — a very low, divided neck line and two thin silk shoulder straps. Would Edward give me such a personal garment? I though there must be some mistake and looked across to him and he gazed back with a dead-pan expression as Aunt Ada, fingering the fine material, continued to enthuse. Then I realised why he had chosen such a gift: it was to please his aunt who would consider the nightgown just the right gift from a newly-married husband. Or perhaps he'd gone into some shop meaning to purchase an innocuous cardigan or box of hankies and the sales girl — she would be young, slim and sexy — had persuaded him to take this, holding it against her lovely body to show him how it *wouldn't* look on me! I found I was disappointed at this last explanation and pleased when I noticed that the box came from a London shop and had been posted to Edward.

Aunt Ada said: 'So that's why you wanted my Army and Navy catalogue, Edward, you naughty man!' and they all laughed, even poor Uncle Lando though he didn't know why. Mimsy brought in the eggs and bacon and we put aside our presents for the time being. Every one had been pleased with what they received. There at the table Edward had changed his tie to the new one I'd bought him and Ronnie had copied him and now wore the psychedelic one; and Aunt Ada and Mimsy had pinned on their brooches with exaggerated gasps of admiration as the morning sun sparkled the 'jewels'. This was going to be a lovely Christmas!

We walked to church, as we always did unless the weather was bad. That morning, at Edward's side my hand on his arm, and with Aunt Ada and Mimsy following, chattering, I felt almost happy: unlike poor Ronnie, I really was a member of a family, the Constantine family. After my parents died I'd been brought up by an elderly aunt who was reluctantly doing her duty, and then there'd been my typing jobs and the flat-sharing period in Plymouth; at no time any real happiness for me; now I told myself I was *almost* happy because I was afraid something would happen to spoil my present contented Christmas-morning glow.

I was right to be cautious! As we sat in our usual pew near the back of the church Aunt Ada whispered to me: 'Tell Edward that the Penloves and Paula are back. They've been in Spain since June,' she told me, 'and I thought they were staying till the spring.' I passed the information to Edward on my other side and followed his gaze to where, farther down the aisle, an elderly couple sat with a young girl. Instinctively I knew this was the girl the neighbourhood had expected Edward to marry, even if he'd had no plans in that direction.

When the service was over and we stood outside the church in the wintry sunshine exchanging seasonal greetings with the villagers, Mr. and Mrs. Penlove and Paula were introduced to me and they were invited to our coming party; then while Aunt Ada and Mimsy talked to the older pair, Paula gave Edward and I an animated loud-voiced account of her stay in Benidorm. She was fair-haired and tall and very elegantly dressed and used her hands a lot to give emphasis to her remarks. 'Then suddenly we wanted to be at home in England for Christmas,' she told us, 'so we flew back last week and I've been busy rounding up the gang for some get-togethers this holiday.' She chatted on and I felt awkward and unable to join in the conversation and was relieved when some more of their friends came to speak to them and we were able to get away.

Christmas was rather spoilt for me after that. I couldn't help thinking about Paula as we ate the customary rich lunch — the turkey had been roasting while we were in church — and during the lazy afternoon that followed.

At tea time we wore paper hats and pulled crakers and everyone was very jolly. Uncle Lando, wearing a scarlet cocked hat, slapped his plate of jelly with his spoon like a two-year-old, scattering it on the table cloth. He was too excited and as usual ate too much; I was afraid he would be sick and was glad when Ronnie took him upstairs. The other four of us played whist in the little sitting-room and then, when Ronnie came down again, family-tradition guessing games remembered by Aunt Ada for the occasion, ending up with a shadows-on-the-wall game where she made hand shadows of animals and we had to guess what they were. 'This was Granny's party-piece,' she told me, 'and I'm doing it in remembrance.' So they *did* think of Granny sometimes: I was glad of that.

We had decorated the rooms with holly and other evergreens but there was no mistletoe: just as we were going to bed Aunt Ada realised this and exclaimed at its absence — she'd had three glasses of port that evening and was a little 'merry'. 'Well, after all,' she giggled, 'Mimsy and me are too old to be kissed and you young ones don't need mistletoe.'

Edward, who had been specially Christmassy-nice to everyone all day, crossed the room to her and said gallantly, 'You're not too old at all, love,' and gave her a smacking kiss which she squealingly pretended to evade. Mimsy had disappeared to the kitchen; perhaps she thought Edward would feel obliged to kiss her too — she was a dear, diplomatic soul, always anxious to avoid embarrassment, for others as well as for herself. When she returned she carried a tray with hot mince pies and more glasses of port. Edward said: 'That's a drink for ladies,' and fetched two cans of beer for Ronnie and himself, and Ronnie, at his chummiest best, raised his glass in a toast to, 'My dear friends at Treworgey!'

'Come, Catherine,' said Edward, thinking it was time to put an end to the festivities, and as we climbed the stairs he praised me, saying, 'Thank you for making this the nicest Christmas we've ever had, my dear.'

'But I didn't do anything!' I protested. 'Aunt Ada and Mimsy made all the preparations.'

'But you were here, Catherine.'

Did he mean that I'd made it the nicest Christmas just by being at Treworgey? He couldn't mean that; he must be feeling the effect of the beer; but I replied, truthfully, 'It's been my happiest Christmas too,' for Paula's appearance on the scene had faded from my mind as the day passed, and in any case none of my Christmasses *had* been so good.

10

The day for the party came ominously closer and I could no longer push it to the back of my mind. It was only to be a cocktail party and would be over in a couple of hours but I had to show an interest and help with the preparations. Mimsy would attend to the refreshments very efficiently though she would probably provide too much, and Aunt Ada would make certain that the big drawing-room was properly aired and warmed and that there were enough extra chairs, but I made it my business to check that the wine glasses were well polished, and the flower arrangements were left to me too — 'You do them so much better than I do, dear,' said Aunt Ada.

On that evening, the evening of the party I dreaded, Edward wore the nice grey suit he had for our wedding and I

139

put on a crimson velvet, long-sleeved dress bought with my allowance specially for this occasion. Paula and her parents were our first guests to arrive and when I saw Paula's slinky sleeveless black cocktail gown I felt dressed like a schoolgirl. And she wore false eyelashes and her lids were painted with gold lacquer; round her neck were five or six long necklaces of bright glass beads; and her evening bag and shoes were embossed with fierce golden dragons. Although she was a blonde she looked like an eastern princess, but I could have forgiven her for being so spectacular if she hadn't also behaved as if she was the hostess: she greeted the guests and moved about the room chatting to each group, making sure they had plenty to eat and drink. I ought to have been grateful to her for she knew these people much better than I did; at first I'd tried to circulate but felt some of the guests thought me to be a waitress hired for the evening, though that was silly of me for if they didn't know me from seeing me in church they'd been introduced as they arrived. Aunt Ada was being no help at all but was closeted in a corner with a couple of the older guests obviously catching up on a year's gossip with them; Mimsy had decided to 'keep in her place' and remained in the kitchen; and Edward, standing by the bookshelf, looked as if he would like to take out a book and read and wasn't making any attempt to be sociable.

I carried him another glass of sherry and then, as we stood there together, Paula came from the other side of the room with a dozen of her friends — well, it couldn't have been so many, there were only thirty guests altogether, but it seemed as many as a dozen to me. They were the younger set who were about her age — and mine, though I felt older — and Paula, smiling at me with her gold-edged eyes, said, 'You hooked Edward pretty quickly! I turn my back for a few months and come home to find I have to cross him off my list! The way you two leapt into marriage one would think you'd leapt into bed together first and there was a bun in the oven!'

I knew my face grew redder and redder, as crimson as my dress. I believed they were all looking at my shape to see if there was a baby on the way, though with legitimate timing for I obviously wasn't far advanced in pregnancy. Perhaps if Edward and I had been sex partners in reality I could have laughed with them; as it was I stood there stiff and silent with shyness and embarrassment.

Edward wasn't bothered by their curiosity, he smiled and joked with them though not in a nasty way; he didn't help me at all, didn't turn the subject of conversation or divert attention from me. When Paula said, 'You must let us know when the heir is on the way, Edward, that will be an excuse for a celebration party!' he replied, 'All in good time, Paula; we're not in a hurry to fill the nursery.' He was good-tempered with their jokes and innuendoes, but when one of the men said, 'After all, there's someone in occupation of the nursery, isn't there?' — meaning Uncle Lando — his mouth tightened and he looked to see who had made the remark, noting the indiscretion.

Paula started to talk about Spain and we moved away to speak to Aunt Ada and her friends. Aunt Ada must have heard what had been said about babies: she whispered, 'Don't take any notice of Paula, dear. She always talks like that, all her set of young people do. I think it's disgusting but it's fashionable nowadays to have everything out in the open and talk about sex and 'buns in the oven'. I feel a little reticence is nicer — though I do hope you start a baby soon, Catherine.'

Aunt Ada too! Why couldn't they mind their own business! Aunt Ada had wanted me to marry her nephew, she seemed not to like Paula, but nevertheless her sort — Paula's sort — would make a better mistress of Treworgey than I was doing, and if Edward had married for love he could have started a family. Somehow I endured the rest of the party-time, trying to be pleasant to everyone; fortunately Paula and her cronies left early to go on to another 'do'. As the others departed in twos and threes, thanking us for our hospitality, I wondered if they really had enjoyed themselves: perhaps they had, the drinks had been adequate and Mimsy's cocktail titbits delicious and plentiful — though was this sufficient for enjoyment?

Because of the party we were to have a late supper instead of dinner; too late for Uncle Lando. He and Ronnie had been kept out of sight this evening, Edward decreeing that Ronnie must stay upstairs with Uncle Lando who would hear the noise of car doors banging shut and extra voices and be restless and must not be allowed to wander down to us or cause any kind of disturbance: he was the Constantine's 'skeleton in the cupboard' though a skeleton with such flesh as his would have been hard to find! As the remaining four of us sat having our meal in the little sitting-room we were discussing how the party had gone and the talk turned to Paula. Hardly believing my ears I heard myself saying emphatically, 'I shall be glad when she's gone back to Spain!'

They stared at me in surprise. I knew it was a silly thing to have said and was so mad with myself I started to cry, I couldn't help it. Aunt Ada, who sat next to me, put a comforting hand on my knee. 'Never mind, dear,' she said, 'you've been working too hard lately, one way and another.' I could tell she thought — and hoped — that my unaccountable tears were the first sign of pregnancy. I stood up and, apologizing for my outburst, said I would go up to bed. Edward said: 'Yes, it's been a tiring evening, I'll come too,' and he took my arm to help me up and gently led me from the room.

But when we were in the privacy of the bedroom he turned to me and said quite sharply, 'Whatever's the matter, Catherine? Why did you behave that way?'

'I don't know,' I replied. 'Somehow I couldn't stop from crying.'

'Oh I don't mean that! You're tired as Aunt Ada said. I mean why did you stand aside and let Paula boss the party? It was *your* party and you should have kept her in her place — as a guest.'

'I was shy,' I told him. 'I'm not used to parties and didn't want us to have one.'

'But it was held specially for you — you don't think *I* wanted it, do you! I'm all for a quiet life and don't care if I see nothing of my neighbours socially.'

'I suppose it was really Aunt Ada who wanted it; she said it was time I met people.'

'Then you shouldn't have let her think you were in agreement, you silly girl! Remember *you* are mistress here, not her. Now we've both had to suffer an evening's embarrassment and boredom; and I doubt if our aunt enjoyed herself all that much, she doesn't like Paula but we had to invite her and her parents, seeing them in church on Christmas Day as we did. Well, never mind, forget about it now, though we have to go to Penlove Place — Paula's planned a party and I've accepted the invitation to it thinking you would want to go.'

'I won't go!' I declared, appalled at the thought of another agonising evening.

'Of course you will go, it would be very rude, and peculiar, to back out now. Do you want them to think you *are* having that baby?'

I gasped; my whole body seemed to gasp at what he'd said; but I repeated childishly, 'I won't go!'

'You will!' he said sternly, not joking, and without saying good-night he crossed the room and shut himself into the dressing-room with a noisy bang.

I undressed and climbed into bed. I

was cold — though the room was warm — and rather frightened. I curled up and pulled the bed-clothes half over my head, glad of the comfort they gave me. I heard the dressing-room door reopen and held my breath, not moving. Perhaps Edward wanted to say good-night or even to apologise for his dictatorial manner, I don't know: thinking me asleep, he quietly closed the door again and thankfully I turned over and drowsily practised imaginary, successful conversations with Paula for the next time we met, for of course Edward had to be obeyed and I would have to go to her party.

11

With the new year came some very mild weather; we had snowdrops blossoming in January and even a few primroses, and Aunt Ada was fearful that such an early spring would bring on the garden plants too soon, for them to be cut back by colder weather later — we hadn't had Tom Pacey's hard winter, not yet at any rate. Meanwhile it was delightful to walk in the woods — the natural woods, not the criss-cross lines of planted-for-timber pines — and hear the birds singing and feel the warm damp air working its magic on the foliage.

Ronnie and Uncle Lando were walking too. 'It will do him good to get a bit of fresh air and exercise,' Ronnie said, and I agreed, for there was something unhealthy about Uncle Lando's flabby pink sugar-fed skin. If I met them in the woods, heralded by

Ronnie's ever-playing transistor radio bought with his Christmas cheque, Uncle Lando would be carrying a handful of specimens: a few of last autumn's acorns, a spray of variegated holly, some ferns or a twig with the scarlet 'moss-cup' fungi — unknown to me till now. He was a child on a nature ramble and Ronnie his school-teacher friend. Apparently one day they went as far as Nanny Bullen's and Uncle Lando came home so excited and happy it seemed as if he would float off into the air like a big balloon.

I hadn't been at Treworgey a year yet and really only knew fully the happenings since the last summer; it was difficult for me to put the past into perspective: of course, Nanny had been Uncle Lando's nurse years ago; had tended him after his accident during the months when it was uncertain how long his illness would last, and then probably into his manhood — in fact till she could give no more help and, instead, needed to be cared for herself:

family servants of her kind didn't retire, they worked till there was no more work left in them.

These two, Nanny and Uncle Lando, had been overjoyed to see each other, Ronnie told me. They had kissed and then sat chatting all the afternoon: I doubted this and thought it would be Ronnie who did the chatting, interpreting for both an invented conversation, for besides the fact that Nanny was almost totally deaf it had taken me a long time to understand her toothless mumblings; and as for Uncle Lando, his sentences were rarely strung together to make sense. However, I didn't doubt their pleasure in each other's company and was pleased at this new interest for them both, and wondered why no one had thought of reuniting them before this chance occurrence.

I worked in the library most mornings — it was now more an office than a room to read in — but I liked to get out for a walk in the afternoons otherwise I was having too much of the company of

Aunt Ada and Mimsy and their knitting: though I loved them, one could have a surfeit of their conversation which rarely moved from things domestic. I spent the evenings with them in the little sitting-room and when Edward joined us there was more to talk about, but Ronnie, when he came down for an hour or two, made little difference, he was so much in tune with them. There was the television too, of course, but their choice of programme wasn't always what I wanted to watch. But in the afternoons I could do as I pleased and on one of my walks when I'd ventured farther into the woods than usual exploring a new-to-me path found I was coming out to a clearing, a gate at the edge of the trees led into a sunlit field — to my surprise I saw Edward, and Jasper, come through the gate into the woods.

Edward hadn't seen me, I was still too far away, and I was just going to call to him when Paula Penlove came from the field to join him. Whatever was

Paula doing here in our woods? Some instinct told me to be quiet — and as I watched they kissed, and kissed again! Edward had his back to me and they were much too preoccupied to notice my presence; their kisses weren't tentative but deep and lasting a long time; Jasper had run away into the field again and didn't get scent of me.

As I hurried back along the path I tried to understand the unbelievable scene I'd just witnessed, but couldn't! Edward had as good as said he didn't like Paula and he'd never seemed a man to lie — only the few white lies and misrepresentations necessary to keep Aunt Ada happy regarding our marriage. Now here he was with Paula — and I already hated her — and very much involved emotionally; and she was the girl the neighbourhood had expected him to marry: perhaps they had good reason to expect it! We hadn't attended the Penloves' party, it was never mentioned again; Aunt Ada had had a bad cold and I thought that had been used as an excuse for our absence; if it was overlooked altogether I wasn't going to remind Edward, I was too relieved at not having to go. Luckily, since the Christmas-morning attendance we'd not seen Paula or her parents in church.

Stumbling along, anxious to put distance between myself and them, I felt sick — physically sick. Edward, my husband, and Paula making love publicly like that! But of course they hadn't been in public but in private woods and had believed themselves unobserved. That didn't excuse them though! Edward had persuaded me to marry him and had made clear the kind of marriage it was to be; he hadn't seemed unsatisfied with the arrangement. The return of Paula must have reawakened his love for her — but what about me? I realised that I was jealous! My doubtful liking for Edward, then uncertain friendship, had developed into love!

I can see it now, I thought, doing a bit of self-analysis: I'd been in love with him for months! I remembered the afternoon he'd rowed me down the creek to see Nanny Bullen and the way his nearness had embarrassed and excited me; and how, on the night of the fire, I'd felt almost as if the end of life had come for me too if he was to die of his burns; and the teasing, bossy way he'd treated me when he was confined to bed had pleased me, really; and the Christmas-present nightie had thrilled me too. Yet all this time I'd also kept to my belief that he was a bullying dictator, unkind to keep Aunt Ada parted from her son, too absorbed with his saw-mill and other affairs and only married to me for his own convenience. I'd had my chance and lost it! Now I could never show him how I loved him. Why had I been so blind! Those weeks when he was in bed had provided plenty of opportunity; although he'd been aggravating there were times when I'd thought he was flirting with me; I could have responded if only I'd had the sense to interpret my feelings for him! I ran part of the way home, hoping to escape from my despairing conclusions.

At dinner that evening I became a nasty detective. I asked Edward if he'd had a busy afternoon and despised him when he told me how one of the power saws had broken and he'd been trying all afternoon to contact the repair men. I looked down at Jasper who sat on the floor beside me waiting for his plate of scraps and I patted his head and asked, 'Did you have a busy afternoon too, old man?' and Edward laughed and said, 'That one won't budge an inch if he can help it. He's been napping all day.' Jasper gazed back at me without batting an eyelid and I thought with disillusion, You deceiving pair!

I was fretful and argumentative all the evening, and I snubbed poor Ronnie when he joined us which made me ashamed of myself, he was so good with Uncle Lando it was mean of me to resent his intrusion. Then when Edward put his hand on my arm as we climbed the stairs to bed I jerked my arm away, avoiding contact. He looked surprised but said nothing.

The next morning I sought out Tom Pacey: I would have been surprised to see Paula in the woods even if she hadn't been rendezvousing with Edward and I wanted to find out where the Penlove estate was; I expect it was another of those things they all thought I knew and Tom was the best person to ask. I couldn't ask Edward now; and I didn't want to arouse Aunt Ada's curiosity, she would wonder why I wanted to know and might even uncover, somehow, Edward's infidelity. That would be awful, she had such faith in him and our married happiness.

I found Tom in the garage washing down the Bentley and after a few remarks about the weather I put my question to him and he told me, 'Penlove Park is next to us, the nearest big property to this one. The land is only divided by the road that runs between, though Penlove Place, the house, is over on the far side of their piece, nearly into Treluz Minor.' I thanked him and returned to the library but instead of doing my book-keeping I thought of the Penloves. Theirs was the next estate to Treworgey! Edward and Paula could meet in the woods easily, secretly, and as often as they wished without arousing comment — and how often *did* they meet?

I don't know how I endured the next couple of months. The weather changed and we had a lot of cold winds but whenever possible I still walked in the afternoons. Frequently I returned to the spot where I'd observed the lovers together: I never saw them again but to me that only confirmed my suspicions that they had a love-nest somewhere — but where? Other times I would walk to the mill, not along the valley road but through the top woods to the clearing where I'd first caught sight of it; I would wait up there, hidden behind bushes which although only just begining to leaf were thick enough to give me cover, and when I saw Edward down there, or Jasper, as I sometimes did, a great sense of relief flowed through me for I knew, that afternoon at any rate, my husband wasn't with Paula. I would have gone there every day to check except that I knew he couldn't always be there, and on the days I didn't see him I was frantic with jealousy — I was afraid of those days and their effect on me. Jealousy, I found, was destructive: some tender, vulnerable part of me, my appreciation of beauty, love of nature — joy of life, perhaps it was — was perishing. I hated the birds that woke me with their song these spring mornings!

I tried to forget my awful secret and behave normally, especially towards Aunt Ada and Mimsy who were so kind to me. They saw that something was wrong but couldn't fathom what it was and as there was no sign of a baby coming Aunt Ada decided this was the trouble and I was pining for one. 'Be patient my dear,' she would urge me.

'There's plenty of time.' I thought it was just as well she should believe me unhappy for this reason as that she should know the truth, though the matter would have to come to light some time, I couldn't go on like this for much longer. Nor could Edward and Paula go on as they were: Edward would have to come to me and 'confess' and try to put things right by asking for a divorce; this, I believed, was the right action to take in the circumstances, even in these 'permissive society' days. Edward didn't avoid me, that would have been difficult with Aunt Ada's eye on us; he was polite and friendly when we were in company but when we were alone he rarely addressed me and I attributed his silence to a guilty conscience.

Nanny Bullen died that spring: she died quickly and quietly, as Granny Constantine had done, without any in-bed illness first. I missed her as much as I'd missed Granny for, although their positions in life had been so different, in a way they'd become the same person to me for I'd not known Nanny till after the death of Edward's grandmother and in my mind they'd merged into one Treworgey old lady. Poor Uncle Lando missed Nanny too, though in recent weeks the colder weather had limited his visits to his old nurse and I wasn't certain if he realised she was dead. But Ronnie said: 'He's really upset, poor boy!' and I squirmed at 'poor boy' for Uncle Lando was twice Ronnie's age: I shouldn't have minded though, for Uncle Lando seemed a child to all of us, we all tried to please and protect him and ignored his foolishness — but small irritations loomed large with me these days.

12

Cornwall in springtime, if the weather is good, is the most perfect place to be; but to me the new-green April leaves, the primroses and first bluebells, and the clamorous bird-song were ironical: this was the time I should have been most happy, loving Edward and perhaps loved by him, and instead the season's beauty mocked me everywhere. I couldn't even be honestly miserable for I had no right to disturb the other occupants of Treworgey just because things had gone wrong for me.

I wondered, since they'd come to church at Christmas, if Paula and her parents would be in St. Cuthberts on Easter Sunday — their church attendance might be at special religious-festival times — but they didn't appear and I wasn't sure if I was glad or sorry for this: with plaguing curiosity I wanted to see Edward and Paula together to note how they behaved in public, yet I dreaded the effect seeing them would have on me. But the next Sunday as we entered the church I saw Paula, looking lovely in a navy linen outfit and a large white, black-banded, 'Princess Anne' hat, sitting alone in their family pew.

After the service I stopped in the church porch to speak to Mrs. Pacey, Tom's wife, who had been ill: this was her first time out of the house for several months and I wanted to ask her how she was and give a little sympathy, and also to deliver messages from Aunt Ada and Mimsy who had not come to church this morning. Mrs. Pacey and Tom had no children to visit them or care how they were in health, and neither was young though Tom was still active and kept working; we regarded them as part of Treworgey.

When I rejoined Edward he was with Paula. They were talking in an ordinary, neighbourly way, cleverly concealing their feelings, and as we greeted each other Paula made a point of being very sweet to me and admired my yellow dress. On the spur of the moment I invited her to lunch with us at Treworgey. Edward looked surprised but seconded my invitation and Paula accepted eagerly: 'I'm at a loose end today,' she told us. 'The parents have flown back to Spain to have another holiday before it becomes too hot down there. I'll phone home from your place to say I'll not be back to lunch.' She turned to me to explain: 'Old Martha, our housekeeper, would fret and wonder where I was,' she said, and I gave her credit for considering the servant. It was funny that although I wanted to hate her — *did* hate her — when I thought of her being kissed by Edward, I couldn't entirely dislike her, and she seemed to like me: she was confident and outspoken, very different from me — perhaps it was the attraction of opposites or, in my case, reluctant admiration for her good looks and personality.

She drove us back to the house in her car and while she used the phone Aunt Ada set another place at the table. There was always plenty to eat, an extra made no complication regarding food, but we weren't used to unexpected guests and Aunt Ada dithered over where to seat Paula and ended up by putting her next to me and opposite Uncle Lando. The meal went very well except that Uncle Lando stared at Paula a lot, and he spilt the mint sauce when passing it to her. The conversation was general, Edward and Paula were being very careful not to reveal any connection other than that of neighbours, then as we started on the dessert Paula surprised us all by saying, out of the blue, 'I'm going to have a pop festival at Penlove Park.'

We looked at her in amazement — except Uncle Lando who was busy with his baked custard. Edward was the first to speak: 'You can't do that, Paula!' he exclaimed.

'Why not?' she retorted, indignant at the shocked way we'd received her news, and I could tell she wasn't used to having her actions questioned. 'It'll be for charity,' she told us. 'I'll send the proceeds to an orphanage or the old people's home. I'm having Gospel Johns and his Followers and I'll book a couple of other singers too. Gospel and the Followers are nice chaps, I met them in Benidorm when they were entertaining there last autumn.'

'They may be perfect specimens of manhood,' replied Edward sarcastically, 'but it's the riff-raff who flock after them — the beatniks and hippies or whatever they're called — that we don't want here. They'll be in the Hawken district for weeks, sleeping rough and hanging about the village begging, borrowing or stealing and generally making a nuisance of themselves! You mustn't bring them here!'

I agreed with him: according to Tom Pacey only the width of a road separated our estate from Penlove Park, there would be trouble for us too — I thought in terms of 'our' and 'us' in regards to the estate. Aunt Ada must have been thinking the same way and she said: 'They're a lazy, good-for-nothing lot, Paula; I don't think you should encourage them. They dress so peculiarly and wear their hair — the men, I mean — right over their shoulders, some of them!'

'Well, so does your Trevor!' retaliated Paula.

Aunt Ada was electrified. 'Have you seen him?' she asked eagerly, forgetting the question of long hair.

'I saw him in Plymouth a couple of weeks ago,' stated Paula. 'He was with that chap who used to work here — wasn't his name Victor?'

'How was Trevor looking? What was he doing?' questioned Aunt Ada.

'If you really want to know,' replied Paula, 'he was down at the Barbican, sitting on a wall, strumming a guitar and making eyes at the girls.'

'Oh dear! I do wish he'd get a job;

start a career of some sort. Did he look well?'

'In the pink,' said Paula, who was becoming bored with the subject of Trevor.

Ronnie, who'd been rather quiet during the meal — I don't think he knew who Paula was and wanted to establish her connection with us — turned to her and remarked: 'I'm fond of pop music, Miss Penlove. Gospel and his Followers are very good performers; we had all their records at the hospital.'

Paula beamed her approval at him and he smiled so sweetly that I was again ashamed for so often finding him irritating: Uncle Lando loved him; Aunt Ada and Mimsy were pleased he was with us, enjoyed his company; was there something wrong with me that I couldn't appreciate him? Then I remembered that Edward, too, had little liking for Ronnie and only endured him because he was so necessary for Uncle Lando.

Edward excused himself from the

lunch table now as Mimsy and I began to collect the plates, and Ronnie and Uncle Lando retired to their upstairs room to prepare for a nature walk or spend the afternoon with coloured paper and glue — they were constructing a cardboard zoo with scarlet lions and purple lambs and exotic birds no eye has ever gazed on. Aunt Ada said to Paula: 'Will you join us in the little sitting-room? We have our cup of tea in there.'

'No, I think not, thanks,' replied Paula. She turned to me and asked: 'Why don't you come for a drive? It's a nice afternoon.'

How could I go riding in her car, she was my enemy! I said: 'No, thanks. I'm going for a walk.'

'Then come with me part of the way. I'll drop you at our west gate and you can walk back down through Fox Hollow and into the woods.'

I could find no reason to disagree with this so we set off. Paula's big hat had been thrown carelessly to the back seat and her fair hair, soft and silky, blew gently round her face as we drove along; she still wore too much make-up but it suited her. I certainly couldn't blame Edward for preferring her to myself.

She took the road into the village and then turned right, a new way for me for we always turned left for Treluz Minor and Major and the Plymouth road. After the outlying dwellings of Hawken were passed the road was really only a narrow track and if we'd met any other traffic we'd have had to draw in to a field gateway to allow it to pass. 'Where does this lane lead to?' I asked Paula, and she replied, 'It's one way home for me but it's the way to the Point too; there was a gun-emplacement — or something like that — out there during the 1914–1918 war; one can still see bits of the old cement base though it's mostly overgrown with heather now.'

'The gun that Granny Constantine saw sink the German submarine, I suppose.'

'Oh yes, I forget you must have known Granny,' said Paula. 'That old girl was a walking history of Cornwall, especially of this part. But she was a selfish old bird! She ruled the roost at Treworgey most of her life and then retired to a comfortable perch.'

This was an opposite picture of Granny to mine: Edward's grandmother had seemed a sweet old lady to me, but then we all have different points of view and Paula and Granny must have fallen foul of each other in some way.

'She warned me off — off Edward, I mean,' Paula told me, confirming my deduction. So was she only enticing Edward to spite his deceased grandmother! But even if *she* wasn't serious Edward must be, for he wasn't the kind to indulge in a casual affair.

When we'd driven for a couple of miles Paula pointed to the right and told me, 'Treworgey territory that side and ours this side,' and a little farther on she stopped the car at a widening of the lane where tall wrought-iron gates, permanently open by the look of the weeds that grew round them, were supported by pillars topped by stone greyhound-type dogs; the dogs had once been smooth and graceful but now were chipped of ear and toe and pock-marked by lichen. This was the first time I'd even seen the outskirts of Penlove Park and it appeared to be a place of decaying grandeur, very neglected. 'Is the house like this too?' I asked, meaning was it in such a state of dilapidation; then I hoped Paula didn't think me rude. But she only laughed and said: 'Why not say, is it as shabby as this? Yes, it is! You must come over and inspect it some time.'

The Penloves didn't seem short of money: why were no repairs done? I suppose Paula could see that I was wondering about it for she explained: 'My parents wanted — and expected — me to be a boy; a son to carry on the name and the estate. They were disappointed, and now the title will lapse with the death of Father; there's no nephew nor even a remote cousin to step into his shoes, so he lets the place deteriorate. He and Mother would rather spend the money on a bit of Spanish sunshine and I can't say I blame them; when the estate comes to me I'll probably have to sell it to pay the death duties, in any case there won't be enough cash for its upkeep.'

'I didn't know your parents were titled,' I said. 'I addressed them as Mr. and Mrs., I'm afraid.'

'They don't mind that — prefer it, I think — but they are 'Lord' and 'Lady'. And I'm Lady Paula though I don't use the 'Lady' except when I'm induced to open a garden fete or bazaar. Father is Lord Penlove when he's being chairman of a meeting or Justice of the Peace but otherwise we're the same as everyone else.'

'Yet your father wanted a son to carry on the name.'

'Oh, that's just family pride; the continuity thing that's in all of us.

Edward will want sons, you know, so you'd better be prepared to produce some.'

She was looking at me, laughing and expecting me to laugh too. How could she speak of such a thing to me! She knew Edward's kisses and caresses herself yet could talk of he and I and love-making!

Paula had taken a compact from the glove compartment of the car and was busy touching up her face, unconcerned with me and my awful thoughts; she didn't know how I was cursing her! And another thing occurred to me: did Edward wish he'd married Paula because through her he would acquire more land, another estate? He should have looked before he leapt! But, although he was more relaxed now, in my early days at Treworgey he'd grumbled at having too much responsibility, too much to do; nor did I think he was a man to seek material self-advancement by way of marriage: my jealousy was making me too suspicious, but I was silly to sit here pretending friendship with Paula and feeling as I did; I thanked her for the lift and got out of the car.

We were on high ground and the view was lovely: first a long, low cradle-shaped field with cows grazing, then our woods in spring-green splendour, then the blue sea. I could just pick out the tops of Treworgey's chimneys and could judge where Hawken Creek was by the break in the trees though the saw-mill was deep down out of sight. Somewhere to the left of the creek must be the cottages where Nanny Bullen and Mrs. Smith had lived — I'd learnt that Edward owned the cottages, which were tumbledown and too isolated to merit repair, and he'd paid Mrs. Smith to live in one of them and look after Nanny because the old lady had wanted to stay where she was: Mrs. Smith had moved back to Hawken village now that Nanny was dead.

Paula, still in no hurry to drive home

through the greyhound-guarded gates, said: 'That's Fox Hollow there; if you go down through the field — you're not afraid of cows, are you? — and past the farm you'll come to Fox Gate and the path in the woods will take you back to Treworgey.'

I looked down into Fox Hollow, to the gate at the far end: there was something familiar about it. Suddenly the geography of this little area became clear to me: that gate was the one I'd seen Edward come through when I was in the woods the other side of it; and Paula had joined him and they'd kissed and cuddled! Fox Gate was their meeting place and Paula dared to bring me this way and tell me to go down there! She must be very insensitive — but of course she wasn't aware that I knew their secret. I coolly thanked her again and she thanked me for lunch and we said good-bye, but she didn't start the car engine to drive away.

I walked slowly down the long field between the grazing brown-and-white cows which were contentedly munching the lush spring grass and took little notice of me; a few had small calves alongside them, nudging for milk. I passed the farm: it was a typical Cornish farmhouse, squarely built of grey stone with a grey slate roof, rather box-like, but with good windows and a wide front door; one corner of the house was covered with a climbing pink clematis; alongside of it were cattle sheds and a big Dutch barn. I was not very close and could stare without being rude.

It was strange to think that in all the months I'd been at Treworgey I'd never visited the farm; had never till now discovered the source of all the rich dairy produce that came to our kitchen. Of course the farm was a different matter to the saw-mill which Edward was deeply involved with and went to nearly every day; it was a separate unit with an efficient manager — whom I'd never met though I'd spoken to him on the phone. Edward had listed the farm among his trials and tribulations but really it gave him little cause for concern.

I came to the Fox Gate and climbed over because it was securely latched to stop the cattle straying into the woods and I was afraid that once open I might not be able to shut it properly. I'd started along the path through the trees when Edward — and Jasper — came round a corner towards me. Was he on his way to see Paula? Was she coming down to meet him? She must be very contemptuous of me, risking discovery like this! But perhaps she wanted me to know of their attachment, wanted to force an issue, hoped I'd start divorce proceedings. What should I do? I'd pretend to think this a natural casual meeting with my husband: I waved — he was still some way off — and shouted, 'Hello Edward!'

He didn't reply but came on towards me. I was puzzled: he couldn't hope I hadn't seen him! Then I realised the man wasn't Edward! Nor was the dog

Jasper! It was Edward and yet it wasn't Edward! This man had the same height and breadth of body, the same colour of hair and eyes, but as he came near I could see the coarser skin, thicker lips, longer nose; and he was older than Edward. But he wore the same kind of clothes as my husband — old trousers and tweed jacket — and could easily be mistaken for him, there under the trees. Of course, this was the man who was trysting with Paula! This man was her lover, not my Edward! My blood bubbled like champagne, my feet danced under me it seemed: I must have appeared crazy to this double of Edward for I was laughing with relief. 'I'm sorry,' I gasped, as he came close. 'I thought you were my husband,' and I hoped he'd think the mistake itself enough cause for my hilarity.

Evidently he knew who I was for he replied with a smile, 'Yes, Edward and I *are* alike, Mrs. Constantine. My name is Derek Northey; I'm the farm manager.'

I wondered if he'd been at Treworgey

when Edward and I had the little party after our wedding: if so, I'd been too self-absorbed to notice him. 'You're so much alike I could have sworn it was Edward coming towards me,' I told him. 'How strange!'

'Well, I don't know that it's so strange after all,' he said. 'My family has farmed here on the estate as long as Edward's family has been at Treworgey, and that's a very long time. Somewhere down the line there must have been inter-marriage or even a bit of illicit love-making and then, generations later, nature shakes up the chromosomes to produce two of a kind almost at the same time. Edward doesn't let it bother him and neither do I; our sameness doesn't affect my work and the way I direct the farm for him, and our lives don't run together otherwise.'

While he'd been giving me an explanation I'd composed myself. Close friends and neighbours would see the difference in the two men, and Mr. Northey's voice was different from

Edward's for he spoke with a strong Cornish accent while Edward, because he was sent away to school as a boy, had no recognizable regional tones in his voice. I looked at Jasper — not Jasper, of course; fatter, but surely a relation of his? Mr. Northey guessed what I was thinking. 'Yes, she's like Jasper. Old Mrs. Constantine, the one that died last summer, came to buy one of my pups for Edward years ago. I breed boxers, you see, and they all turn out much the same; this is a younger dog, of course.' I remembered Edward telling me that Granny had given him Jasper as a birthday present; this dog must be a niece or great-niece to Jasper — if that's how dog relationships go. I stooped to pat her but she was suspicious of me and growled, and Mr. Northey said: 'Best not to make a fuss, her pups are due at any moment. And she's the aggressive type — is taught to be.' Apparently the corpulence was unborn puppies; I asked: 'What's her name?' and he replied, 'Rosa.'

We wished each other good-afternoon and as I walked on I wondered what he thought of Paula's pop festival plans and the possible trespassers his dog might be required to chase off the farm, which was the closest part of Treworgey land to Penlove Park.

But Paula's lover was not my Edward! I hurried home as if on air!

When I saw Edward at Sunday supper that evening I wanted to fling my arms round his neck, to hug and kiss him and tell him I loved him and would never doubt him again — but how could I do that? As yet we'd hardly touched each other except when he gave me his arm in public formality and, when he'd been ill in bed, I'd helped him to take food and drink; and in any case at the moment we were further apart than ever because of my withdrawn behaviour due to what I thought was his love-making with Paula: I must be careful, not take things too quickly.

The conversation naturally turned to

the proposed pop festival. With Paula not there it was possible for Edward and Aunt Ada really to give vent to their indignation and concern; Mimsy gave an occasional murmur of agreement, Ronnie stayed silent, Uncle Lando was only interested in the food, and I said nothing particularly in favour of or against the project till an extra-strong condemnation of Paula from Edward made me burst in with, 'Oh, for goodness' sake let her have her festival!' I was so happy myself I could afford to be generous to Paula.

But of course this was the wrong attitude for me to take, it made me seem irresponsible. Edward and Aunt Ada began to explain the bad effect the festival would have on the village, and perhaps on Treworgey, though I was well aware of the disadvantages and couldn't tell them that now I knew Paula wasn't misbehaving with my husband I didn't care what she got up to. To change the subject, I asked, 'Why didn't any of you tell me that the

Penloves were titled people?'

Aunt Ada replied: 'I didn't think to mention it, dear. It's one of those things one believes everyone knows.' And Edward said: 'Come, Catherine, is this the reason you're suddenly in favour of the festival? Don't tell me you're a snob and *Lady* Paula can do no wrong!'

'Of course not!' I declared indignantly. 'But I wondered if what she does is any of our business?'

'Of course it's our business! And the business of all Hawken!' he answered, getting up from the table as if too disgusted with me to stay there.

Instead of closing, the gap between us was widening!

13

Just after lunch a few days later I received a telephone call from Paula; she always spoke rather loudly and on the phone nearly shattered my ear drum. 'You seemed interested in the house on Sunday,' she shouted. 'Why don't you come over this afternoon and have a look round.'

I wasn't sure if I wanted to go or not so I prevaricated with, 'I don't see how I can; it's too far to walk, isn't it?'

'It *is* a long way,' she replied, 'but there's the Bentley; let Tom Pacey drive you over, it'll give him something to do.'

Give Tom something to do! How little Paula knew of our regime at Treworgey if she thought Tom needed occupation: I sometimes thought he worked harder than any of us; besides, he was past retiring age and could be taking things easy now except that he was the kind of man who was happiest when busy.

Unable to evade her invitation I agreed to go over to Penlove Place and then was worried in case Edward wanted Tom or the car that afternoon. I phoned the saw-mill and asked Edward if I might use the Bentley and he replied, 'Of course, Catherine!' as if he thought me silly to ask. Foolishly, I didn't tell him where I was going.

Half an hour later I was driving away from Treworgey with Tom. Although Tom and I were friends and I visited his wife in their home near the church; and although he and I sometimes worked in the garden together and had long chats about Granny Constantine, old times at Treworgey, and the continuing happy existence of the saw-mill cats; when we were out in the Bentley I had to sit in the back of the car and be the mistress of Treworgey and he was our chauffeur — he would not have it otherwise. Now, as we drove through Hawken, he asked:

'Which entrance to the Park would you like to go in at, ma'am?'

'Oh, the main entrance, please. I've never been that way,' I replied. So instead of turning towards Pen Point and the west gate to Penlove Park we drove straight on for a couple of miles till we came to a little hamlet that Tom told me was called The Gates; the cottages, at the entrance to the Park, had all been occupied by Penlove employees years ago, Tom said, but now, with the changing times, some were rented by Hawken people and some were derelict. Here were taller pillars than at the west gate, and bigger gates, and larger stone greyhounds, and two small empty-looking lodges, but the state of decay was the same; and there was a curved, pot-holed drive with wide grass verges and an avenue of horse-chestnut trees with here and there a tree missing or blown down and not dealt with that gave the impression of a mouth of teeth needing attention. As we came to the house the drive divided to circle a fountain overgrown with moss: here marble nymphs danced round a giant dolphin which spouted water into a shallow cockle-shell pool.

The house itself was not as large as I'd expected, or as the once imposing entrance suggested, but it was a beautiful place of old grey stone — Georgian, I thought — and again neglected. Tom drew up outside and handed me out of the Bentley. I sent him home, feeling there was no sense in keeping him waiting, perhaps for a couple of hours, or in asking him to come back for me — he would find it tedious to be in his best dark suit all the afternoon, unable to work for fear of getting it dirty. I would find my own way home; if I wanted an excuse to escape from Paula I could say there was the long walk back to Treworgey.

A wide flight of steps led up to a balustraded terrace and the front door looked never to be opened nowadays, and in fact Paula came out to greet me through a small door at the end of the terrace — a tradesmen's door? 'Welcome to Penlove Place, the decaying home of the decaying gentry,' she said sarcastically: I thought that if this was my home I'd either be more regretful for its demise or would try to bring it back to its former state.

She took me on a tour of the house: first to the kitchen where I was introduced to Martha, the housekeeper, a red-cheeked, motherly type of woman who obviously adored Paula; then to the bedrooms which were a mixture of old — antique — furniture that had been here for many years and colourful rugs and ornaments brought back from foreign holidays; then to the downstairs rooms. The furniture in the main drawing-room was covered with dust sheets, and Paula said: 'You didn't come to my party at the new year or you would have seen this room in all its glory!' Again she spoke mockingly and I wondered if she was putting on an act and in fact *was* regretful for the shabby state of Penlove Place; as we'd gone from room to room I'd noticed patches of damp staining the walls and a musty smell, and everywhere was evidence of the ravages of time, and wear and tear, without reparation. 'The best pictures have been sent to Sotheby's to raise a bit of cash, though I'm afraid we had no Rembrandts or Rubens,' Paula told me, knowing I could see the squares on the walls where paintings had been removed. 'But we kept them till after the party,' she continued. 'We had an absolutely fab time! I wish you had come.' I could imagine it and wasn't sorry to have missed the event.

We had tea on the terrace. The once white garden chairs and table needed repainting. Martha brought out a tray with a silver teapot, and the china was probably Crown Derby; there were cucumber sandwiches so small and thinly cut that it was difficult to make more than one mouthful of them, and rich Dundee cake that Paula cut into huge chunks as if in defiance of the insubstantial sandwiches. She wore a large-brimmed, airy-fairy sun hat and the perforated fabric spotted her face with flecks of sunlight making it seem she had a million freckles — she had offered me a hat too, but my skin never became red in the sun.

Sitting there on the terrace with a lovely view out over the green park I could imagine myself on a stage in a twenties-period play and expected a hero in blazer and flannels to burst from the drawing-room french windows with racket in hand and enquire, 'Anyone for tennis?', or to come snorting up the drive in a dashing two-seater of the time with a girl in a cloche hat and flying silk scarf. Paula said: 'This terrace will be just right for the festival, won't it? The girls and boys will be able to see Gospel perfectly, looking up at him.'

When Paula said 'girls and boys' she made her pop festival sound a harmless teen-age party and I wondered if we were wrong in condemning it as we did, but I was already in trouble through seeming to give the affair my approval so I said, 'Edward's very much against your holding the festival; wouldn't it be best to give up the idea and save a lot of bother?'

'Why should I, it's no business of his!' she exclaimed. 'He's a fuddy-duddy!' Then seeing my look of indignation at her name-calling, she added: 'You're very much in love with him, aren't you?'

'Of course I am!' I declared, implying that I had been from the beginning and ignoring the fact that I'd only just discovered my love for him.

'Ah well, young love and all that!' she mocked.

'I'm not so very young,' I protested. 'Nor is Edward.'

'That's true — and nor am I, come to think of it.'

I thought a bleak look came to her face as if her parties and pop stars and holidays in Spain hadn't brought happiness. 'I'll have to be getting back now,' I told her, standing up. 'Thank you for the nice tea.'

She laughed. 'You sound like a child saying 'thank you' after a party, as her mummy has taught her to. I'll come part of the way with you — you'll go the west gate road, I suppose?' The west gate road that leads to our farm and Mr. Northey! I thought; but in fact she only came far enough to set me in the right direction.

It was a long straight road, through grass-land without trees, and the sun blazed down on me: I wondered what this area would be like when the festival was in progress for Paula had told me it was here that there would be what she called the 'facilities' — refreshment tents and toilets, I suppose she meant. She had chosen this spot because the ground was level, and the west gate was the easiest way into this part of the Park for the transport of food and other necessities, but Edward would take her decision to have the main goings-on close to the Treworgey estate as deliberately done to be a nuisance to him.

I came to the greyhound gate, crossed the lane, and was going down through Fox Hollow when I saw Mr. Northey; I didn't really want to encounter him again so soon but couldn't turn back. He saw me and waited: 'Good-evening, Mrs. Constantine,' he said, and I noticed that, as on Sunday, he didn't address me as 'ma'am' as many of our employees did, and he called Edward by his Christian name — of course as farm manager he had higher status than most of the people who worked for us. 'Good-evening, Mr. Northey,' I replied, and for want of something else to say I added, 'You haven't got Rosa with you today.'

'No, she's had her pups,' he told me, smiling with pleasure. 'Would you like to see them?'

'Oh yes please,' I said, feeling it would be churlish to refuse his invitation, he was so obviously enthusiastic himself.

I expected to be taken to an old

stable amongst the outbuildings or, since he was a dog breeder, to proper kennels, but to my surprise he led me into the farmhouse itself. There was a dark hall with a wide staircase and four downstairs rooms with open doors; and in one of the back rooms, a kitchen-cum-living-room, Rosa was lying in a basket under the table, ecstatically happy with her three new puppies. She was too proud to be doubtful of me today, and I made a fuss of them for her master's sake and for her own, though I preferred cats to dogs, then I didn't quite know what to do; I'd seen the puppies but couldn't rush straight out. I knew Mr. Northey was a bachelor, and knew from the wage sheets that a number of men came from the village to work at the farm — I'd heard the clatter of milking-time as we came up to the house: was a housekeeper employed too? 'Do you live alone?' I asked.

'Yes, and I do my own housekeeping except for a woman who comes occasionally to give the place a good cleaning. My parents died years ago; they were elderly parents anyway — I mean I wasn't born to them when they were young. Father was manager for Edward's grandfather. This is a photo of my parents.' He took a passe-partout-framed photograph from the mantelshelf and handed it to me: it was a picture of a middle-aged, homely pair — Mr. Northey wasn't like either of them. 'They are nice,' I said, handing it back; then unthinkingly, not meaning to emphasize his solitude, I asked, 'Aren't you lonely, living in this big place by yourself?'

'No,' he replied. 'I have Rosa and the other dogs, and dogs are good companions. Besides, all of us are on our own really, you know. We may laugh and cry, quarrel or make love with other humans but basically we are alone.' What a cold philosophy, I thought, for I'd been so lonely myself in the past and had been so happy at Treworgey, and would be again now I knew that Edward wasn't in love with Paula and might come to love me: I was unsociable by nature but I didn't want to be alone again. A clock in the hall began to strike and I realized it was time to be getting home. Mr. Northey came with me as far as Fox Gate. As we parted he said: 'Call in any time you are walking this way, Mrs. Constantine: living near-by all my life, naturally I am interested in the affairs of Treworgey and I'm glad you are there; it's nice for Edward to have someone young about the place, not just his aunt and uncle' — he made no reference to the fact that the uncle — Uncle Lando — was unable to play his proper part in our lives, and I thought that kind of him.

As I hurried through the woods I looked at my watch: it was ten past seven — ten past *seven*. I'd believed the farm clock was striking six o'clock, and that was late enough! Wherever had the time gone? We dined at seven and I would be late! I hastened along as fast as I could.

I'd reached the clearing, a sort of cross-roads in the woods where paths branched off, when Edward appeared, coming from the garden. He was angry — relieved to see me, but angry! I loved him but was a little afraid of him too, and wished I could disappear behind the trees.

'Where have you been, Catherine?' he demanded. 'I was terribly worried! Do you know how late it is? You drove off in the Bentley and told nobody where you were going and I had to find out from Tom Pacey that you went to Penlove Place! Why go hob-nobbing with Paula just at this time when we're opposed to her festival ideas! And in any case, even walking home, you should have been back before now. I was afraid you'd turned your ankle or were in some other trouble.'

I think his anger was a reaction from his fears for me. I explained that I'd also been to the farm but that made matters worse. 'Really Catherine!' he stormed. 'As if it wasn't bad enough for you to visit Paula that you must go to Derek Northey's too! Why choose those two, of all people!' He forgot that I hardly knew anyone in the district; we led isolated lives at Treworgey.

He hustled me through the garden and straight to the dining-room; the others had started their meal. 'We couldn't keep Lando waiting,' apologized Aunt Ada. But Uncle Lando beamed at me and so did Ronnie and Mimsy, and Edward made certain my food was hot: I was forgiven, but not any nearer to winning my husband's love.

14

Paula continued with the preparations for her pop festival which didn't surprise me for she'd booked Gospel Johns and his Followers before she spoke of it to us, and in any case the argument at our lunch table was unlikely to deter her — rather the opposite, for she was used to having her own way and had resented the criticism — nor was my half-hearted attempt to dissuade her when I was at Penlove Place for tea likely to have had any effect. Besides Gospel, the programme now included Wes Wills and Dinkie Dee: we learnt this from the colourful posters that now stared at us from every available space, such as barn doors and telegraph poles. We didn't know who was responsible for this unlawful bill-posting but I believed Paula quite capable of pasting up these herself.

Tom Pacey told us that the villagers had mixed views regarding the event. At first many had thought it a good idea to have a crowd come to the Park: there would be extra trade for the Hawken shops and the pub — the Penlove Arms — and it was amusing to read about the arrangements in the local paper, about the extra police being brought in and the first-aid tent being erected; there had even been an item on the radio with some of the residents' opinions recorded. But as the actual date came close and the road from Plymouth thronged with hitch-hikers trying to thumb lifts, and as the verges became over-night camp sites, and then as the village itself became choc-a-block with hippy-type youngsters who — it was thought — would rather steal than buy, and who — even if it was otherwise — looked dirty, there were very few left in favour of the festival. I suppose the young people of the village looked forward to the excitement, life in Hawken was dull for some, but there was so much talk of drug taking and sex orgies — real or imagined we didn't know — that even they must have been nervous of participation in the festival goings-on.

I hadn't encountered any of the hippies myself, but as I didn't care for their kind of music or the outlandish clothes they wore, and was alarmed at their reported bad behaviour, I would be glad when the affair was over and done with. Except for Ronnie who, I think, wished he dared to be one of them, and Uncle Lando who was unaware of what was happening, we at Treworgey agreed about this. At lunch one day Edward said: 'Derek Northey has had trouble at the farm. The hippies are crowding up at the west gate entrance to the Park and that night we had the gale-force wind they couldn't keep their tents up and decided it would be a good idea to take to Fox Hollow for shelter. I told Derek to send them packing or they'll be into the woods and up to all kinds of mischief!

The boat has disappeared from the saw-mill beach so it looks as if they've already been down that way!'

Remembering — how could I forget! — that Mr. Northey was Paula's lover, I found myself asking: 'Is Mr. Northey in favour of or against the festival?'

'Against, of course!' declared Edward, as if no one connected with Treworgey could be in favour, and forgetting that Ronnie enjoyed pop music and that at one time it had been supposed that I supported Paula too. I wanted to speak about the likeness between Edward and Mr. Northey: Mr. Northey had agreed that they were alike and said it didn't bother either of them but I wondered if Edward *did* find it irksome. He obviously wasn't in a mood to be questioned so later on when we were having our after-lunch cup of tea in the little sitting-room I spoke to Aunt Ada about it instead. I said: 'I met Mr. Northey for the first time the other day, Aunt Ada. He and Edward are very alike, aren't they?'

'I suppose so,' she replied, treating

the similarity as unremarkable: there could be no dark family secret of illicit love needing to be kept hidden. She added: 'Of course Edward is much more handsome.'

'Of course,' I agreed: I was very willing to accord that Edward was the better-looking of the two. I happened to look over to Mimsy who was pouring me another cup of tea and saw that she was smiling: dear Mimsy, she herself probably thought her employer more handsome than Mr. Northey, but was amused at Aunt Ada and I and our convincement of Edward's superiority; for thinking our man the best. As I grinned back at her, admitting preju- dice, I wondered if she'd ever been in love. Mimsy was more sensible than Aunt Ada in some ways and had more humour; was she happy with a life of cooking and cleaning and caring for us at Treworgey? These two were very fond of each other, it was a life-long friendship from their schooldays, as they'd told me; had this female partnership been enough for Mimsy; was she content always to second Aunt Ada's views? 'What do *you* think of this pop festival business?' I asked her.

'Well, of course we don't want the crowds here,' she replied, 'there's so much hooliganism and vandalism nowadays, but I suppose most young people are restless or dissatisfied, or anxious to put the world to rights, and each generation expresses itself in a different way. Today it's pop music and what they call the 'drug scene'; with us it was the Eton crop and the Charleston and smoking cigarettes — in our day it was a very naughty thing for young girls to smoke. We were the flappers of the nineteen-twenties: I don't think our elders and betters had much patience with *us*.'

'*Did* you dance the Charleston, Mimsy?' I asked unbelievingly.

'Indeed I did!' she declared, putting down the teapot and doing a shoe-shuffle on the carpet to prove it.

'Then give me an exhibition, both of you,' I pleaded.

Giggling, Aunt Ada joined Mimsy and together they danced a spirited version of the Black Bottom with Aunt Ada humming the tune and adding a couple of 'Boop-a-Doop's. Instead of two middle-aged women, one plump and the other tiny, with wrinkled skin and greying hair; wearing out-of-fashion too-long dresses; I saw the pair of lively schoolgirls they had been — daringly modern, with all their adult life ahead of them and confidently looked forward to. As, breathless and laughing, they flopped on the settee, I clapped enthusiastically. I envied them: these two had had fun, had enjoyed their teen-age years, whereas for me that time — my own teen-age time — had been difficult and drab and lonely. Perhaps none of us should begrudge the young their pop festivals: neither those who had enjoyed their own kind of fun belonging to the period, nor those who, like me, felt cheated.

The festival was to be a four-day

event. On the first day as I walked in the garden I could hear the music, not a recognizable tune but the beat of rhythm that came throbbing through the still air of the hot June morning; it was frequently interrupted by noisy, screaming applause. That evening there was an item about the festival on the television, in the local news. We all watched it, even Edward: we were shown the crowds in the Park, then close-ups of young people lying on the grass in the sunshine listening attentively to the music or making love unmindful of onlookers. There'd been a lot of stripping off of clothes, it was so hot, and Aunt Ada gasped at the nakedness — some, even girls, were naked to the waist! The extra police had made a search for cannabis or other drugs, we were told. 'Whatever is the world coming to!' exclaimed Aunt Ada. Yet in one interview a nice young couple said that hippies were gentle people; that they shouldn't be condemned just because their sense of values was different from 'straight society'. They were a religious pair and spoke of God as if he was with them, there at the festival. Personally I felt that religion and pop music didn't mix well, but if this was their way of boosting faith it was all right with me as long as they behaved themselves. But, of course, few were there for religious reasons, and some not even to appreciate the music but for a noisy, youthful get-together and a bit of sky-larking thrown in.

On the evening of the second day we were shown — on the television screen — Paula and Gospel and Wes Wills on the terrace steps. Despite the heat Paula was wearing a striped poncho and long boots, but looked strikingly attractive; the performers had skin-tight pants and floral-patterned shirts — we couldn't tell the colours on our black-and-white set but I guessed they were startling. Paula didn't do things by halves and had her arms round Gospel and was kissing him and teasing his beard with her long fingers, perhaps for the benefit of the cameras. There was a bit of recorded chit-chat and then the interviewer asked if the festival was a success. 'More than I dreamt! Absolutely super!' declared Paula, and then, when it was suggested that by many in the district the audience was regarded as an 'unwashed and unwelcome nuisance', she added: 'Let the old fogies say what they like, these are sweet people who only want to listen to music in peace!' As she said this last sentence she seemed to be looking out of the set straight at us. 'She wants some sense drummed into her!' fumed Edward, and Aunt Ada added, 'Or her bottom smacked!' Obviously there were two points of view on the matter of pop festivals: on which side was I?

Paula was entertaining the performers — entertaining in the sense that she was providing board and lodging — for the duration of the festival and was holding a big dinner-party for them the last evening — we'd politely declined our invitation to it. Now as she paraded on the terrace steps she said to the interviewers and photographers, 'You can all come to my party, we're going to have a fabulous time!' Then as the television camera gave us a last sweeping view of the scene I thought I saw Trevor with a group round the nymphs-and-dolphin fountain; the cockle-shell pool was being used as a washbasin. I looked to Aunt Ada to see if she'd noticed but her expression of deep disgust hadn't changed: perhaps it wasn't Trevor or perhaps she hadn't recognised her long-haired son.

15

As the weather continued fine and the festival continued noisy we were relieved to hear of another festival to take place up in Devon somewhere the next week, for this meant that the Penlove Park audience would remove themselves to the new locality. Paula's festival youngsters had become out of control, even by the extra police, and there'd been gang fighting in the night and some village windows broken; there was also a shortage of food and water at the Park and we heard that Paula had handed out her special food when it was delivered by the caterers and abandoned her farewell party. That last morning, when some of the gathering were already packed up and edging the roadside to thumb lifts, Ronnie came to the library and asked to speak to me. 'Yes, come on in, Ronnie,' I said. 'What was it you wanted?'

He stayed near the door as if doubtful of his welcome and I knew I ought to be kinder to him, not let him feel nervous. 'Come on, Ronnie,' I jollied him. 'Out with it! What have you been up to?' This was out of character from me and didn't suit him either for he kept his manner respectful as he asked: 'Would it be possible for me to have the afternoon and evening off? I'd love to go to the Park for the last of the festival!'

I was now quite out of sympathy with the festival and found it ridiculous for a man of his age to want to join that phrenetic mob, most of whom were teen-agers, but I couldn't refuse permission — he only needed to ask for time off, not what he could do in that time. Besides, he rarely left Treworgey but spent the days that were supposed to be his own in continuing to look after Uncle Lando — he planned little treats, picnics and garden treasure-hunts, for his charge — I don't think we valued this enough.

'Yes, that's quite all right,' I told him.

'The trouble is,' he said, 'I can't take Mr. Lando there, it wouldn't be a fit place for him.'

'No, of course not,' I agreed. 'I'll take care of him — from two o'clock?'

'Yes, thanks,' he replied, and added, 'It's one of his sensible days.' He gave me a radiant smile, as if by making it possible for him to attend the festival I'd granted him entry into paradise, thanking me again as he left the room.

After lunch I went upstairs to collect Uncle Lando, distracting his attention from Ronnie's departure by admiring the paper flowers they'd been busy making that morning. He wanted to wear a huge pink paper rose so I helped him into his red-and-white striped blazer and then pinned it in the lapel; this top room was stuffy and I was going to take him for a walk even if we went no farther than the garden.

It was almost unbearably hot down there too, but Uncle Lando insisted on exploring every path — he always appeared to be seeing even very familiar things for the first time. Then, for shade, we went into the woods, just as far as the 'cross-roads' clearing where three other paths started — one led to Pen Point; one, eventually, to Fox Gate; and the third was the path to the pine woods above the saw-mill. Last month this clearing had been thick with bluebells but now these were dead and, instead, we were circled with white flowering rhododendron bushes, the blossoms early over-blown for we badly needed rain. Uncle Lando and I sat on an old wooden seat which was in the shade of an oak tree, and soon my companion had slipped down so that his head was supported by the seat-back and was asleep; I felt sleepy too.

Then I noticed that Jasper was behaving strangely — he often followed me round now instead of chasing out to jump in the Land-Rover with Edward; he was an old dog with little energy this hot weather. I watched him walk slowly into the bushes where he laid down awkwardly, his belly on the grass, as if his legs wouldn't hold him up; then he was violently sick. Something had upset him and he'd got rid of it, but he would be better back at the house in the care of Aunt Ada. I looked at Uncle Lando — would he be all right if I left him? He was still asleep, gently puffing breath through his half open mouth; a tiny dribble of saliva trickled down his chin; he was like a baby, innocent, contented, unaware of the world's iniquities, but nothing could hurt him in the short time it would take me to carry Jasper to the house.

I picked up the old dog and comforting him with, 'Never mind, poor old boy!' took him back through the wood and garden and into the kitchen of Treworgey. He wanted some water and I filled his bowl with some fresh from the tap; he had a long drink then retired to his basket: he looked better now.

I expected to find Aunt Ada and

Mimsy in the little sitting-room but although their after-lunch tea tray was there the room was empty; they were probably gone to their bedrooms for a nap though it was unlike Mimsy not to have washed the cups first. I thought Aunt Ada ought to be told that Jasper was off-colour yet was it fair to disturb her? She and Mimsy had come back tired after a morning's shopping in Treluz Major; really it had been too hot for them to go but Aunt Ada didn't like her weekly routine upset and today was 'shopping day' — usually the outing was much enjoyed by both.

I went up to the first landing and tapped gently on the door of Aunt Ada's room and then, when I received no answer, on Mimsy's door. She called a faint, 'Come in,' and I entered. She was lying on her bed, her face very white; there was an eau-de-cologne smell throughout the room, and when I asked in alarm, 'What's the matter! Are you ill, Mimsy?' she replied, 'Ada and I have both been terribly sick, Catherine.

Suddenly, almost at the same time, after lunch. Ada is all right, she took a dose of chlorodyne and I expect she's asleep; and I'm getting better every minute, don't worry.'

'It must have been something you ate,' I said. 'What did you two have that the rest of us didn't? And Jasper's been sick too; that's why I came back to the house.'

'We had cream cakes with our morning coffee in Treluz Major. Our own cream from the farm is so lovely yet Ada always orders and enjoys cakes with that fluffy mock cream. I expect that upset us, the hot weather made it turn bad in us perhaps. As for Jasper, he's often been sick lately but I think that's only his old-age digestion playing tricks.'

'Well, as long as you've been sick I expect it's all right. Do you think I ought to phone the doctor, to be on the safe side?'

'No, I'll be up and about again in a few minutes and I'm sure Ada's all right. You look in and see for yourself.'

I left her and crossed the landing to Aunt Ada's room. She was lying on her bed sleeping peacefully and for the first time I saw in her closed eyes and relaxed chin some resemblance to her brother, Uncle Lando — Uncle Lando! I'd forgotten all about him!

I hurried downstairs and out through the kitchen again. I ran across the garden and down the woods path. I didn't want Uncle Lando to wake up and find me gone, he might think himself abandoned, he was never left alone out of doors. Breathless, I reached the clearing: the seat was empty — he was gone!

How long had I been away? Longer than I'd intended, of course, but surely not so very long? I looked at my watch — it was nearly four o'clock and that meant I'd taken more than an hour! Perhaps Uncle Lando had woken up and, feeling hungry, judged it to be tea-time and found his way back to the house — but I hadn't seen him there nor in the garden. I stood wondering what to do; if he had wandered off which way would he go? He would take the path to Pen Point and Nanny Bullen's cottage of course! Ronnie had said this was one of his sensible days, he would remember the way but not realize that his old nurse was no longer waiting to welcome him — he knew she was dead, but did he know what death was? Without Ronnie to direct him elsewhere the path would draw him like a magnet! I ran down the path as fast as I could to catch up with him before he reached the cottage; he would be shocked and disappointed by its emptiness.

I blamed myself for leaving Uncle Lando alone, yet excused myself too, for I'd not reckoned to find illness at the house and would have been back quickly but for that. And it was so hot and Uncle Lando had been asleep: I hadn't expected him to stir. And a big fat man like he was couldn't have gone far. But I didn't catch him up and began to think he'd not come this way after all and when I reached the cottage I meant to just look inside and then turn back.

But at the cottage instead of emptiness I found signs of recent habitation. The windows were broken and the door half off its hinges but a fire had been burning in the grate — perhaps the night before — and the room was littered with old blankets and sleeping bags. A tea-chest table held dirty mugs and a loaf of bread and a pot of jam; and various items of male clothing — socks, underpants, T-shirts — were strung across the room on a make-shift string line. A guitar was propped against the wall. Pop festival hippies must be using this place as a shelter. There was no sign of Uncle Lando till as I looked round at the mess and muddle I spotted his pink paper rose, the one I'd pinned to his jacket that afternoon, lying near the door.

He *had* been here! And where was he now? Had the hippies been at the cottage when he arrived? What had happened to him? As I stood outside the cottage puzzling what to do I heard voices and laughter coming from the creek. I dashed through the garden and down the path towards the water; breathing was difficult, I'd run too much already. As I came out of the trees I saw a group of youths, a dozen or so, gathered on the weed-grown jetty; they were looking at something in the water and throwing stones. As I drew near I recognized one of them as Trevor and another was Victor, and I wasn't very surprised. With my heart thumping alarmingly I pushed my way between them and there was Uncle Lando sitting in Edward's boat! — his pear-shaped boat that had been missing. It was floating out into the river with its terrified occupant, and the hippies, beatniks, drop-outs, or whatever they were, were jeering and cat-calling. Poor Uncle Lando was frantic with fear, shrieking in his high-pitched voice, and as we watched he stood up! I knew the boat was sturdy; and the water was smoothly calm, like dark green glass, and looked as if one might walk on it; but Uncle Lando was a big man, and balance was not one of his strong points, he often tottered on dry land; and he was in a bad state of fright! The boat overturned and as Uncle Lando, clutching at air, was tipped into the water it drifted slowly away towards the middle of the river.

At once Trevor ripped off his trousers and dived in off the jetty. A couple of the others followed him. Uncle Lando was flapping his arms in an attempt to swim — I expect as a boy he'd been able to swim — and he *could* have been saved, but, of course, as soon as his nephew reached him he hung on to him for life and with that weight pulling him down Trevor didn't have a chance — neither had a chance.

I directed one of the boys to run to the saw-mill for help, showing him the lower path through the woods parallel with the river; then with Victor — who told me he couldn't swim — and the others left there I clambered down to the small pebble beach like the one at the saw-mill jetty and we waded out as far as we dared. The swimmers who had followed Trevor had now, by diving for the bodies, got hold of Uncle Lando and Trevor and were bringing them in, and we gave what assistance we could.

It all happened so quickly! From the moment I'd discovered that Uncle Lando was missing to this moment seemed no time at all. As I stood there watching Victor and the others trying to rid Uncle Lando and Trevor of water and start their flooded lungs to work again I turned to a boy who stood beside me, one who'd hooted and jeered with the rest but, like them, was now shocked and sober-faced, and asked: 'What happened?'

He shivered — we were all cold and wet now — and replied: 'The fat man came to the cottage and we teased him a bit; Trevor told us he was silly in the head. He ran away and we chased him down here and he climbed into the boat.' The boy looked at me shame-facedly: 'He got into the boat himself,' he emphasized, as if this might excuse them a little. 'The boat drifted out a short way, to the reach of the rope that tethered it, then Trevor cut the rope and it floated on out into the river — but we could have got him back! If only he'd stayed still and not panicked we would have swum out and towed him in!'

I said nothing: this wasn't the time for condemnation nor was I guiltless myself. But they'd teased and tor-mented a harmless, affectionate, lovable simpleton; a grown man but with hardly more sense than a two-year-old, who could neither understand their horseplay nor know how to evade them! The situation had got out of hand and now nothing could put things right again. I gazed at Uncle Lando's body lying on the beach — they'd abandoned attempts to revive him and were concentrating on Trevor — and, strangely, he looked happy; there was no mark of terror on his face, just the simple, trusting smile of expectation he gave us at table when starting a meal.

But Trevor was awful! White, bloodless, with dark black shadows widening under his eyes and round his mouth. He seemed very young; just a boy. Could he have supported Uncle Lando, even a calm Uncle Lando who kept his head? If it were not that he was responsible for the accident he would be regarded as a hero to have attempted rescue.

I heard the Land-Rover, with the engine racing angrily, forcing its way along the narrow path. As it came to a stop at the top of the beach Edward jumped out and ran towards us. Victor gave up his resuscitation work on Trevor and told us, 'It's no use! He's gone too!' Edward examined the two bodies and agreed that there was no hope of reviving either; then he listened to explanations of the drownings. He turned to me: I suppose I was looking rather bad, I was cold and wet and very shocked; he held out his arms and I took a step towards him and that is all I remember — I lost consciousness.

16

I was ill for more than a month. I'd raced through the woods to the cottage and then down to the jetty; I'd had the traumatic experience of seeing Uncle Lando and Trevor struggling in the water, drowning; then watched the attempts to bring them back to life, standing there icy cold after being too hot, and all the time feeling responsible for the circumstances yet unable really to give help: I must have been on the point of collapse when Edward arrived on the scene.

As I lay in bed weak and delirious I saw Edward and Aunt Ada and the doctor standing round me, and I seemed to be with them too, looking down on myself. Someone said: 'She's had a terrible experience: in a way it's a good thing for her to be ill like this, it will give her a chance to come back to reality slowly. Keep her on these tablets, they'll give her some peace.'

Whether this was really said or not, I don't know, but much later on Edward told me my illness had been a blessing in disguise for Aunt Ada too. He said: 'She nursed you day and night, and while she was so worried about you there was no time to grieve over Trevor and Uncle Lando. I was amazed that she could be so practical: her son and her brother were beyond help but you were alive and needed her — and she loves you dearly.'

By the time the iron band of pain across my chest had eased and I was able to eat more than just invalid sops the inquest and double funeral were long over. Even Victor and the remnants of the pop festival, Trevor's friends who'd remained to give evidence, were gone from the district and the Pen Point cottages had been reduced to rubble, for Edward was determined they should not be used by any delinquents or lay-abouts who came our way in the future.

I blamed myself bitterly for Uncle Lando's death; if I hadn't left him alone in the woods he would still be alive; but, I found, nobody else blamed me, they all blamed themselves. Edward said he should have taken more care, should have made certain there was never a possibility that Uncle Lando could wander off by himself, and that he ought to have checked that none of the festival people were on the estate. Aunt Ada said: 'If only I hadn't insisted on having those cream cakes! Mimsy didn't want to, but kept me company so that I wouldn't look greedy. None of this would have happened but for me and those cakes! Catherine would have gone straight back to poor Lando if I'd been there when she brought Jasper in.' And Ronnie, poor man, felt the most to blame of all though I considered he need have nothing on his conscience. He remained at Treworgey while I was ill, helping with the chores and sorting and disposing of Uncle Lando's clothes and 'toys'. He had truly loved his charge and had been happy with us and took the inevitable termination of his employment — he was no longer needed, of course — as a kind of deserved punishment.

The day of Ronnie's departure was the day I lunched downstairs for the first time since the accident. It was awful sitting at the table with no Uncle Lando there! The others had become used to his empty place but I hadn't: I missed the shining full-moon face; the pathetic attempts at conversation when his unfinished sentences floated away on air, out of reach of understanding by himself or us; even the slobbering way he had eaten his food, for what would that matter if only he were back with us! A year ago when Granny Constantine was alive there'd been seven at table together: now, after this meal, we would only be four.

After lunch we said good-bye to Ronnie, thanking him and promising to keep in touch, though I wondered if we would. We waved to him as Tom Pacey drove him off in the car, then Edward put his arm round me and said: 'Come, Catherine, back to bed now, this is enough excitement for the first day,' and I obediently let him take me upstairs. I was happy to do as he said, to have his protecting arm round me, to feel I was loved — for I was beginning to believe he *did* love me.

One day when I was still resting in bed afternoons Paula visited me. She talked a while, not touching on the tragedy, then she said: 'I'm restless. Nothing goes right for me! I shall join the parents in Benidorm; perhaps I'll open a boutique and stay out there. Father writes that he's thinking of turning over Penlove Place and the Park to the National Trust.'

Without considering what I said, I enquired: 'If you do stay in Spain, what about you and Mr. Northey?'

'How did you know about that?' she asked. Then without waiting for a reply she said: 'That was only our animal appetites getting the better of us. He needed a woman and I needed a man. We kept it up for a couple of years, whenever I was home, but it's over now and it won't matter if we never meet again. I suppose you know that he and Edward are related? Their likeness gives it away, doesn't it! Derek is Granny Constantine's illegitimate son.'

I was astonished, unbelieving; I may have had my mouth open in surprise for Paula took one of the traditional-gift grapes she'd brought me and popped it in my mouth. 'It was after Orlando's accident, when his pony tossed him,' she continued. 'Apparently Granny wasn't very affectionate towards her eldest son, Edward's father, nor to Ada whom she always rather despised, but she absolutely idolized Orlando and when he was turned into an idiot she nearly went crazy herself. Her husband sort of retired into his shell like a snail, the other two children went back to their boarding-schools, and I suppose she was lonely and unhappy and she had an affair with old Mr. Northey at the farm — when I say *old* Mr. Northey I mean Derek's father. She must have been in her middle forties then and I expect she thought she was 'safe' but she became pregnant. They managed to keep it a secret somehow and when the baby was born Mr. and Mrs. Northey, who were middle-aged and had no children, took it and passed it off as their own — well, it *was* his of course. That baby was Derek, and that's partly why when Granny warned me off Edward I went after him instead, to annoy her; because he was hers too, and even closer, being a son not a grandson.'

'But they couldn't have kept a thing like that secret!' I objected.

'They could in those days,' she maintained. 'It was a long time ago; both Treworgey and the farm were isolated, more then than now, and perhaps the Treworgey servants kept their mouths shut to keep their jobs — there was a lot of unemployment at that time.'

'Does Edward know?'

'Oh yes, I expect so; and Ada and people like old Tom Pacey and his wife; but they all think they're the only ones who know so the matter never comes up to the surface for discussion. I shouldn't mention it if I were you.'

'Oh I shan't!' I assured her. 'It's none of my business' — or yours, I thought. I wondered if the tale was true or if she'd invented it — and believed it, too — because of her spiteful dislike of Granny Constantine. It seemed incredible — impossible — yet this would account for the similarity, the almost doubling of features, that had been enough for me to mistake Derek Northey for Edward. But even if the story was true it was not for me to bring it into the open: I would never speak of it unless others did.

Paula, feeding me another grape, said: 'I envy you. There was a time when I thought I might marry Edward though he didn't look my way, but you are the right sort for him, the long-loving and faithful kind, and I couldn't have guaranteed to be faithful. He will love you for ever and never go off the rails himself, and although he'll want you to fill the nursery, you won't mind that I daresay.' She leant over and kissed me. 'Good-bye,' she said. 'If I weren't going back to Spain I think you and I could have been friends.' She filled my mouth with yet another grape, squeezed my hand and departed.

With the petting I received from Aunt Ada and the specially tempting foods prepared for me by Mimsy — though there was nothing wrong with my digestion — I was soon quite well again: soon according to how ill I'd been, for I learnt that I'd been very ill at first; pneumonia had developed from the strain of so much running and getting so hot and then so cold. So one morning, feeling fit again, I decided to be done with the lazy life and start to pull my weight again at Treworgey; I knew Edward was in the library so I went to present myself for work. He was spending a lot of time at the house now, and Aunt Ada had told me that when I was most ill he had rarely been out, and always on his return the first thing he did was to check how I was. At the library door my thoughts were carried back to my early interviews with Edward when I first came to Treworgey and, being in memory back in those days, I unthinkingly knocked on the door and waited for his 'Come in,' before I entered. He was seated at the desk and Jasper was on the hearthrug just as on my first morning here.

'Catherine! Why ever did you knock!' he scolded me. He plumped up the cushions in the easy chair but I didn't sit down. I said: 'I thought it was time I took over the book-keeping again. I'm quite well now and have been lazy not helping before this.'

Edward ignored the matter of book-keeping as if he'd never heard of it. He was looking at me thoughtfully, then he said: 'Let's go for a stroll in the garden, you need plenty of fresh air and sunshine to help you feel properly well, and I want to talk to you — let's go down to the lily pond.'

The french windows were open so with Jasper following slowly behind us we walked through the garden to the secluded, overgrown pond — perhaps this was a favourite garden place with Edward as it had been with Granny. We sat on the half-circle seat with the high privet hedge behind us. Edward was silent so to reopen the conversation I asked: 'Shall I start work tomorrow morning — after breakfast like I used to?'

Edward lounged back against the seat, his arm behind me, lightly holding me. He said: 'There's no need for you to do so much of the book-keeping now, you know; you've set the accounts straight for me and I find it much simpler to keep things up-to-date. I've been wondering if you'd like to go away for a while, for a holiday; a change of scenery would do you good.'

So that was how he wanted things to

be! I was wrong in thinking he might love me: he was fed up with me and I was to be banished for a 'holiday'; then, probably, I would be told to stay away for ever!

'Don't you like the idea?' questioned Edward, watching my reaction to his suggestion. He added: 'The mill is running quite smoothly and in any case we close for the summer holidays in a fortnight's time. I could easily risk being absent for as long as a month; we could go abroad somewhere, if you'd like that; we never had a honeymoon so one is due to us, you know.'

'You mean *both* of us to go? Oh yes, I'd love it!' I replied, happy and excited at the prospect, and over-joyed that he wasn't sending me away in disgrace.

'Really Catherine, you're a strange girl! I've loved you ever since you came here and one minute I think my case is hopeless and the next I think I'm making progress with you at last! I thought we were getting on well together at the time of the fire and at

Christmas, then suddenly you seemed to loathe me, couldn't even bear for me to touch your arm; I was right out of your favour this spring and I blamed myself for insisting on our marriage, you were so unhappy.'

'I mistakenly took Derek Northey for you when I saw him kissing Paula, and it was a long time before I found I was wrong,' I explained.

'Oh there's no knowing what Paula gets up to!' He dismissed our neighbour as if she didn't matter at all, nor did he show any interest in the doings of his double — his uncle, if Paula's story was true. He gazed enquiringly at me and I turned away, suddenly very shy. 'Do you mean you were jealous?' he asked. 'That's wonderful! Just the reaction I would have attempted to create if I'd known!' His arms came tightly round me, and tighter as I tried to wriggle away; then he was kissing me — deep, searching kisses that compelled me to respond. Miraculously, he loved me! And had loved me even before we married and in spite of my being so awkward and uncertain and unattractive. 'You are so lovely!' declared Edward, between kisses, as if he had read my thoughts, and I sighed, blissfully happy, and enjoyed his attentions: it was lovely to be loved!

Later, as we sat cuddling and whispering together — though there was no one to hear us — Edward said: 'I knew I was taking a risk when we married, you might never have come to love me, but you kept on about going back to Plymouth and I felt I would lose you for ever if I allowed that; yet I thought I would frighten you away, that you would scuttle off like a scared rabbit, if I became amorous too suddenly, you obviously hadn't considered me as a lover. I decided the best thing to do was to persuade you to marry me, then the rest could come later — it's taken a long time! When did you first know you loved me?'

'I don't know — perhaps the first time I realised it was when I thought I saw you with Paula in the woods. I came back that day feeling the end of the world had come; disgusted with myself for not having known I loved you, furiously jealous of Paula, and angry with you for kissing her instead of me! Then when I found out my mistake and was eager to show how I loved you, you were cross with me about the festival, thinking I should have been more opposed to it, and I believed *you* couldn't love *me*.'

'You'll have to get used to me being bad-tempered sometimes. I'm accustomed to being boss at the mill and round about the estate and can't easily slip out of it when at home. Just ignore it and remember I love you.' He kissed me again. 'Shall we go in and start our honeymoon?' he asked. 'I've been longing to try out that double bed with you in it!'

I pulled away from him — shy, coy, schoolgirlish. 'We can't!' I objected: 'Aunt Ada will wonder what's wrong if we go up to bed at this time of day!'

'Aunt Ada, my dear, will be delighted to see it. She thinks I've been impatiently abstaining from love-making since you became ill. Anyway, it's time I proved that we're as happily married as she believes.' He stood up and gave me his hands, persuading me to my feet. Teasingly he played with the zip fastener of my dress, pretending he couldn't wait to get me indoors, 'Come, Catherine!' he said.

THE END